Frosting
and
Friendship

ALSO BY LISA SCHROEDER

It's Raining Cupcakes

Sprinkles and Secrets

I Heart You, You Haunt Me

Far from You

Chasing Brooklyn

The Day Before

Falling for You

Frosting and Friendship

by LISA SCHROEDER

Aladdin
NEW YORK LONDON TORONTO SYDNEY NEW DELHI

ALADDIN
An imprint of Simon & Schuster Children's Publishing Division
1230 Avenue of the Americas, New York, NY 10020
First Aladdin hardcover edition September 2013

Jacket design by Karina Granda

For information about special discounts for bulk purchases, please contact
Simon & Schuster Special Sales at 1-866-506-1949
or business@simonandschuster.com.
The Simon & Schuster Speakers Bureau can bring authors to your live event.
For more information or to book an event contact the
Simon & Schuster Speakers Bureau at 1-866-248-3049
or visit our website at www.simonspeakers.com.
Interior design by Karin Paprocki and Karina Granda
The text of this book was set in Mrs Eaves.
Manufactured in the United States of America 0813 FFG
2 4 6 8 10 9 7 5 3 1
Full CIP data is available from the Library of Congress.
ISBN 978-1-4424-7396-6
ISBN 978-1-4424-7398-0 (eBook)

For my friend Lindsey Leavitt,
who pointed me in the right direction
by sharing her baking disaster stories.
You are the best.

Chapter 1

apple-blackberry pie

BECAUSE BOOK CLUBS DESERVE THE BERRY BEST

On a scale of one to ten, I am a zero when it comes to baking. I've tried, but it seems like every single time, something goes wrong. Here are just a few examples of some of my kitchen disasters.

In fifth grade, I misread the recipe and added a tablespoon of salt to a batch of sugar-cookie dough instead of a teaspoon. I'd planned on giving a plate of pretty, decorated cookies to my teacher for a holiday gift. It was a good thing we sampled them first. I gave her a coffee mug instead.

In sixth grade, my school had a bake sale to raise money for new computers in the library. I tried to make a decadent layered chocolate cake, but when I put the layers together, the cake was so uneven, it looked like the Leaning Tower of Pisa in Italy.

And then there was the time I helped Mom make a lemon cake for a meeting at our house. It looked really dark on top, but we figured some powdered sugar would fix that problem. We later discovered the bottom of the cake was even darker than the top. As in, black. The next time Mom had a meeting, we bought cupcakes.

My mom says she doesn't have the baking gene either, so I shouldn't feel bad. But I do. It seems like every girl I know loves to bake and is an expert at whipping up delicious treats.

My sad skills in the kitchen are the reason I'm secretly freaking out about the discussion going on right now in Sophie's living room. There are five girls and their moms here for the first meeting of the mother/daughter book club that Sophie decided to start. I was so flattered when she asked if my mom and I would like to be a part of it. Sophie and I have been good friends for a few years, ever since we met in theater camp, but we don't go to the same middle school, so it would have been easy for her to leave me out.

Sophie has been explaining to us how the club will work. We'll meet the first Sunday of every month and take turns hosting the club. In addition to the meeting place, the hostesses will provide a list of discussion questions and delicious snacks.

Wait. That's not exactly right. I believe Sophie's exact words were "amazing, delicious, out-of-this-world homemade snacks."

I raise my hand.

"Lily?" Sophie says.

"So, we can't buy snacks?" I ask. "Like at a bakery or grocery store?"

Sophie's best friend, Isabel, replies. "Sophie and I have talked about the snacks a lot. I know we're all busy, but we'll be taking turns, so each of us will only have to bake for the club two or three times a year. We really think homemade treats will make the meetings extra special. We can even exchange recipes, if everyone's interested."

I glance sideways at my mother to see if she's freaking out as much as I am, but my mother is the Queen of Calm. If she's bothered by their homemade requirement, her face doesn't show it.

I take a deep breath and try to copy my mom. She's keeping her eyes focused on the speaker. Her lips are upturned in a slight smile. And her hands are folded in her lap.

Then I give myself a pep talk. My dad taught me this trick because he says there are times in life you need one and the only person available is yourself. I believe this is one of those times.

Lily, stop freaking out about the snacks! Geez, it's not like someone's in the hospital or something. So many people have bigger things to worry about. Get over it. You'll make something and it will be fine. It might taste horrible. Or be black around the edges. Or require a steak knife to cut into it. But it'll be fine.

Sophie continues. "I told my mom that next to seeing friends once a month and reading good books, sharing yummy snacks was at the top of the list as to why I wanted to start a mother/daughter book club. The book club gives us girls a reason to play around in the kitchen and try new recipes. It'll be fun, right?"

I watch as the three other girls nod their heads in agreement with Sophie. I remain calm, all the while thinking how awesome it would be to have a book club with pizza delivered at every meeting.

Sophie looks at a piece of paper in front of her before she says, "Okay, I think I've covered everything. After we discuss *A Wrinkle in Time* this afternoon, we'll choose books for the rest of the year while we eat our snack."

One of the girls I just met today, Dharsanaa, points to the pie on the coffee table. "What kind of pie did you make? It looks really good."

"It's apple-blackberry, and I hope it's good," Sophie replies. "It's the first time I've ever made a pie. Mom helped me with the crust."

"And Jack gave you a few pie-baking tips, right?" Isabel asks. Sophie nods while Isabel explains. "Jack is a friend of mine who lives in Seattle. His mom owns Penny's Pie Place, so he knows a lot about pies."

"Yeah," Sophie says. "He told me to wrap the edge of the pie crust up with aluminum foil the last twenty minutes, to keep it from getting too dark."

Isabel rubs her hands together. "I can't wait to try it, Soph. It looks like something out of a magazine."

"But first we have to eat the jam sandwiches," Katie says. "Like Meg and Charles did in the book, the night of the storm."

"We're going to have hot cocoa too," Sophie says.

"Are we ready to start the discussion?" Dharsanaa asks.

"What about a name for our club?" Isabel asks. "Remember, Sophie? We were going to see if anyone had any suggestions."

The fifth girl, Katie, raises her hand. "I have an idea. How about the Baking Bookworms?"

Sophie and Isabel squeal at the exact same time. "I love it!" Sophie says. "It's perfect! Is that okay with everyone?"

I look at my mom again. She looks at me. The Queens of Calm have vanished from the room. We are the Princesses of Panic, because now there's no denying that this club is going to be as much about baking as it is about reading. But everyone is talking and agreeing that it's the best name ever, so neither of us says a word. I try to think of something else, a different name they'd love just as much, but my mind is completely blank.

Sophie's dog, Daisy, barks, asking to be let in from the backyard. Sophie's mom is in the kitchen getting the hot cocoa ready. "Is it okay if I let her in?" I ask.

"Oh, sure. Thanks, Lily."

I go to the back door and open it, and Daisy is so happy to see me. It's started to rain outside. That's probably why she wanted inside. She follows me back to the living room, where I rejoin everyone. Daisy sits near the coffee table and licks her chops as she eyes the pie.

"Oh, no you don't," Sophie says. She picks up the pie and walks toward the kitchen.

"Let's go around the room and assign a month for hosting," Isabel says. "I'll take April. Lily, you get May, Dharsanaa hosts in June, and in July, it'll be Katie. Is that okay with everyone?"

We all nod our heads. I tell myself two months is

plenty of time to find a delicious recipe and practice making it a hundred times. Oh my gosh. Does that mean I have to eat it a hundred times? Maybe my sister will help me. She's athletic and always hungry.

Or maybe we can read a historical book when it's my turn to host. Something from back in the days when sugar was expensive and most people couldn't afford to bake anything really fancy. My great-grandma told me that when she was a little girl she'd get an orange and a few nuts in her stocking at Christmastime and she'd be thrilled. I need a book like that. Then I could serve oranges and nuts and call it good.

Except Sophie wasn't satisfied with just serving hot cocoa and jam sandwiches. She had to go above and beyond what was in the book and bake a beautiful, complicated pie.

I am so doomed.

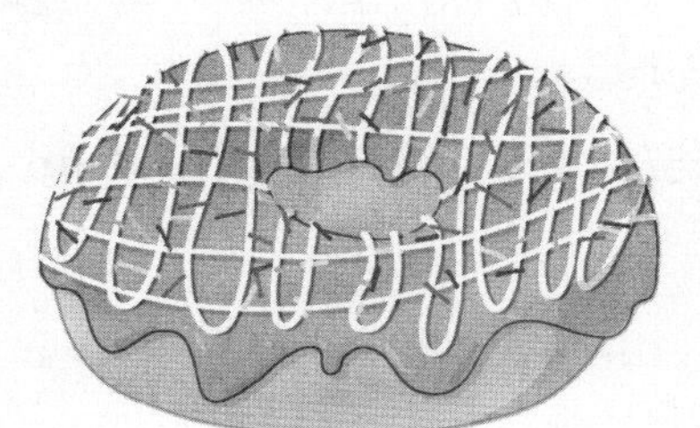

Chapter 2

chocolate-chip-cookie-dough cupcakes

DEFINITELY IMPRESSIVE

"The girls seem really nice," Mom says to me on the drive home. "And their moms too. I think it's a good group. They seem to enjoy baking more than we do, but that's all right. We'll do something simple when it's our turn. I'll go to the bookstore this week and buy the next two books."

We stop at a light near the cupcake shop, It's Raining Cupcakes. The shop is dark since it's closed on Sundays, but I remember how adorable the shop is inside, with the mural on the wall and the large glass cases filled with pretty cupcakes. I wonder if Isabel and her mom know how lucky they are to be able to bake treats that everyone loves. Next month, when it's Isabel's turn to host the club, she'll probably serve the most spectacular cupcakes, like chocolate-chip cookie dough or caramel Oreo. Everyone will *ooh* and *aah* over them. A month later, it'll be my turn. The girls and their moms will go from being dazzled to being disappointed.

"Lily, are you all right?" Mom asks.

"I guess so. I was just thinking how I wish I could be a good baker like Isabel. Did you know she won the baking contest in New York City a few months back?"

"Yes, I did," she says as the light turns green. "And while it's impressive, you have to remember, you have other talents. It's impossible to be good at everything. That reminds me. When are your bandmates coming over to practice again? Have you worked out a regular schedule?"

"They're coming over tomorrow night. We don't have a schedule, but I'll ask them about it at practice. We really want to try and find a party or event where we could perform, so then we have something to work toward, you know?"

Mom pats my leg. "Honey, I think it's great that you girls have taken the initiative and formed this band. I'm proud of you, and I know your father is too. But if I were you, I wouldn't worry about performances right now. Focus on playing together. Write more songs. Have fun. Make it about the music."

I sigh. "You sound like Dad."

"Well, he should know. He's been a musician for a long time, right?"

"But, Mom, our dream is to perform for other people. What's the point of practicing if there's no performance to look forward to?"

"Lily, I'm not saying it won't ever happen. But you've only been a band for a couple of months. You have a lot of years ahead of you. For now, focus on the music. Practice because it will make you better musicians. Isn't that what is most important? Becoming the best band you can be?"

"Yeah. I guess so."

I still don't think there's anything wrong with looking for a chance to perform for other people. There's this other band, the New Pirates, made up of a few kids from school, and they're already performing. Zeke Bernstein's parents hired them to play at his Bar Mitzvah party. Belinda McGuire is the lead singer of the New Pirates. Every time our choir director, Mr. Weisenheimer, has us compete for a solo performance in choral practice, it comes down to Belinda and me. She's a really good singer.

To be honest, I don't like Belinda McGuire very much. It seems like she thinks she's better than everyone else. Maybe she is, as far as her talent goes, but it makes her come across as stuck-up.

Someone else who has a lot of talent is my sister, who jumps out from behind the bushes holding a basketball just as we pull into the driveway. She's talented in all things athletic—and now, at almost giving us a heart attack. Fortunately, Mom is a slow driver.

"Good grief, Madison," Mom mutters under her breath.

"Sorry," my sister says as we get out of the car. "The basketball got away from me and I didn't hear you pull up."

"Look before you leap next time," Mom says, walking toward the front door. "Dinner will be ready in an hour, girls."

Mom goes inside while my sister, Miss Show-off, twirls the ball on her pointer finger. Her short brown hair is matted to her face and her cheeks are all red. She's probably been out here shooting hoops most of the afternoon. "How was the book club?"

"It was all right."

"Do you guys have a name?" she asks me, now doing some fancy dribbling move between her legs.

"Do you ever get tired of showing off?" I ask.

She grins. "Not really."

Yeah. That's what I thought.

"Come on," she says. "You must have come up with a name, right?"

I don't want to tell her. She'll make fun of it the second I say it. But she'll find out sooner or later. "The Baking Bookworms."

She stops dribbling and laughs. "When they taste

something you make, you'll have to change your name to the Burnt Bookworms."

I knock the ball out of her hands before I turn to go inside. She scrambles after the ball rolling toward the bushes again. As I approach the front door, I hear her running on the pavement and, a couple of seconds later, the ball swooshing through the net. No doubt a perfect shot.

After I hang up my coat, I head to the family room. The television is on and Dad is just getting up out of his chair, holding his guitar with a broken string hanging from it.

"Hey, Lily Dilly," he says. "Your mom said the book club was fun."

"Yeah. I guess so."

He squints his dark brown eyes at me. "That doesn't sound very convincing."

"Did she tell you that baking seems to be just as important as reading in this club?"

"No, she didn't."

"I really like the girls in the club," I tell Dad. "And I want them to like me. Sophie and I have been friends for a quite a while, but sometimes it feels like I'm second best to her other friends, especially Isabel. This book club is my chance to show Sophie I fit in, you know?"

He pats me on the shoulder before I take a seat on the sofa. "It'll be okay. The most important thing is to have fun. And the more you practice, the better your baking will be. You know, because practice makes . . ."

He wants me to say "perfect." I think it's his favorite saying. I'm sick of the saying myself. "Makes delicious brownies?"

He laughs. "You betcha." He walks past me. "I need to fix this thing since I have a gig tonight. See you at dinner." He flashes me the peace sign, which is his way of saying "see you later." My dad is cool like that.

"Okay, Mr. Peace. See ya."

I pick up the remote and flip through the channels, trying to find something good to watch. I stop when I see a round man with bright red hair and lots of freckles on his face holding a fork. There's a piece of cake on a plate in front of him, and after he takes a bite, he exclaims, "Sweet Uncle Pete, that's good!"

He sets the plate down and smiles at the camera. "I hope you enjoyed the lesson today on how to make a decadent coconut cake. Please tune in to *Secrets of a Pastry Chef* next week, when I'll show you how to bake a white-chocolate-raspberry cheesecake. This is Chef Smiley signing off. Remember: With the right tools and the right attitude, baking is a piece of cake!"

I immediately program the DVR to record the series.

Mr. Smiley, where have you been all my life?

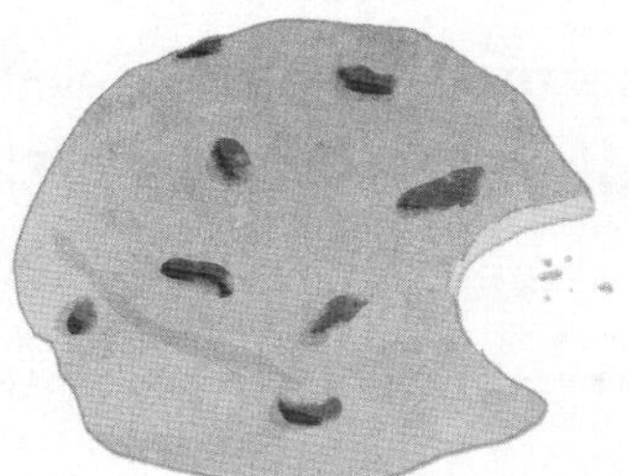

Chapter 3

salted-caramel-mocha cupcakes

SWEET YET SOPHISTICATED

The next day at school, my friend and band-mate Abigail is waiting for me at my locker, her wavy red hair pulled back into a ponytail with a green ribbon around it. Green is her favorite color. She's wearing a cute T-shirt with a picture of an owl. It says I'M A HOOT.

"Your hair sure is getting long," I tell her as I go

to work on my locker combination. "I'm surprised your mom hasn't cut it off yet."

"She really wants to, actually. Said she has a new style she wants to try out on me." She reaches over and pats my straight brown hair. "Hey, maybe I should volunteer you to be her guinea pig. You'd *love* a new style, wouldn't you?"

I shake my head hard. Abigail's mom is going to beauty school. She decided she was tired of working in retail and wanted to become a hairstylist. "You know I haven't changed my hair in, like, four years. Why should I start now?"

"Maybe it's time for a new look. A new Lily! Something that screams rock star."

I laugh as I pull out my algebra textbook and notebook. "We're not really a rock band, are we? More like a pop band."

We walk toward math class, which we have together. "We need to come up with a name," Abigail says. "How can we be a real band without a name?"

"I know. We should work on that tonight."

"Tonight?" she asks, looking at me. "Are we practicing tonight?"

"Abigail, did you forget? Seven o'clock. My dad's playing every night this week at the Wallflower, so we can use the studio as much as we want."

We stop outside the classroom, waiting for the bell to ring.

"Hey, girls," we hear behind us. "How's it going?"

We turn and find Belinda flanked by the other Pirates, Bryan and Sydney. Belinda always dresses like she's about to go on stage. Today she's wearing a purple miniskirt with a black blouse and black boots. My mom would never let me come to school dressed like that. I look down at my jeans and pink Converse sneakers and realize I wouldn't *want* to come to school dressed like that.

"Have you heard the news?" Belinda asks, twirling one of her blond corkscrew curls around her finger. She's got more curls than a toy poodle.

"What news?" Abigail asks.

"Mr. Weisenheimer convinced Ms. Presley to let some local talent perform at the Spring Fling."

Every April, our middle school has a Spring Fling on a Friday night for the seventh and eighth graders. They set up games in the gym, like badminton and

Ping-Pong, and some of the classrooms have activities like a cakewalk, bean-bag toss, and bingo. There's music in the gym, too, usually with a DJ, and kids can dance if they want to, although most of us just stand around with a soda in our hand and talk while we listen to the music. A few kids who are amazing dancers might go on the dance floor to show off what they can do, but that's about it.

"What do you mean by 'local talent'?" I ask.

"From our school," Sydney says. "They're going to have tryouts and let someone, a singer or a band or whatever, perform a few songs on stage."

"Pretty awesome, right?" Bryan says as he swings his head back to get the bangs out of his eyes. I have to say, I am a little bit envious that Belinda is in a band with Bryan. He is so cute. He keeps talking. "We already know what song we're going to do for the audition."

I swallow hard. "Audition? When's the audition?"

"We don't know yet," Belinda says. "They're supposed to let us know sometime this week." She smiles a big, fake smile. The kind of smile that says, *I look forward to beating the pants off you in that audition.* "Think you guys will try out?"

Abigail starts to reply. "I don't—"

"Of course we will," I say. "Yeah, we're all over that. We have some great songs. One of them is *really* awesome. It's the kind you can't help but dance to, no matter how shy you might be."

Abigail looks at me like I've lost my mind. "Which song is that?" she asks.

I nudge her with my elbow. "Remember? That one song? Um, what's it called?" My eyes dart around, looking for something to say, and land on Sydney's T-shirt, which is pink and glittery and has a big cupcake on it. "The cupcake song. Remember?"

Abigail pinches her lips together, like she's trying not to laugh. My eyes beg her to keep her ridiculous thoughts to herself. She nods. "Oh. Right! The cupcake song. Yeah, it's really fun." She tells the New Pirates, "If you guys come to the dance, we'll teach you how to do the cupcake dance too. How's that?"

Belinda laughs. "Oh, you've made up a cupcake dance to go with the song? Wow, that's impressive, since cupcakes don't really do anything but sit there and look cute."

As if a cupcake song wasn't bad enough, now we've

promised them we have a dance to go with the song? Oh boy. This is worse than a bunch of my mom's friends eating burnt lemon cake that I made for them.

The warning bell rings, thank goodness. The three turn to head to class, but not before Sydney says, "I doubt you'll get to show us your dance. Because we're gonna own that audition. I promise you, the New Pirates will be the ones performing on that stage at the Spring Fling."

"Whatever," I mumble as Abigail pulls me into class.

We take our seats in the back row.

"Really, Lily?" Abigail asks me. "The cupcake song? What are we, six?"

"Hey, cupcakes can be sophisticated," I say, trying to convince myself just as much as Abigail. "What about coffee-flavored cupcakes? I had this salted-caramel-mocha cupcake one time, and it was so good. I wonder if they use real coffee when they make them."

She waves her hand in front of my face. "Earth to Lily, Earth to Lily. That's enough about cupcakes. What about our band? Do you think we can beat the New Pirates?"

"I think it depends on when the auditions are and how long we have to practice," I say.

Immediately after the second bell rings, our principal, Ms. Presley, comes over the intercom with Monday-morning announcements. She talks about a disaster drill we'll be doing in the next few days and an assembly we have coming up on Friday. I doodle in my notebook as she rambles on.

"Finally, plans are under way for our Spring Fling, coming up on Friday, April twelfth." I sit up straight and listen. "Our choir director, Mr. Weisenheimer, and our band director, Ms. Adams, have decided it would be fun to allow a student or group of students to perform at the Spring Fling this year. Auditions will be held after school in just a few weeks, right before spring break, on Thursday, March twenty-first. A group of teachers will choose the act they believe to be the best fit. Good luck, everyone!"

I look at Abigail and give her a thumbs-up. Three weeks is plenty of time to get a song or two ready.

Isn't it?

Chapter 4

peanut-butter cookies

IT'S EASY TO SING THEIR PRAISES

The doorbell rings right at seven. Mom is in her office on the phone, lining up houses to show to a client tomorrow. She's a real estate agent, so she works a lot. She loves her job, though—helping people find their dream homes.

I hurry to the door and find Zola there, holding her drumsticks. Dad has a drum set in his studio that he lets us use, but Zola likes to use her own sticks. She says using someone else's drumsticks is like using someone else's toothbrush. Ew! Her parents bought her a drum set for Christmas last year, when she was one of the students selected to play drums for the school band. She's really good. When kids try out for the drums, the band teacher looks for kids who can pick up a rhythm really quickly, and Zola blew everyone away with her performance the first time she played.

"Hey, Lily," she says.

"Hi, Zola. Come in. Abigail isn't here yet."

Zola is one of the most popular girls at school. She is cute and fun and it seems like everything she does, she does well. Kind of like my sister. When Abigail and I asked her if she'd like to join our band, I was so nervous, but I shouldn't have been. She was really excited that we'd asked her, and happily said yes.

"I love your shoes," I tell her. "I didn't know they made polka-dot ones."

"Yeah," she says, looking down at her purple sneakers. "I think they're kind of a new thing." She looks over at my pink ones. "Dude, you should get yourself some."

Zola says "dude" a lot. Maybe because she has three older brothers. I don't know, but I don't mind. I kind of like it.

I lean up against the staircase. "Do you think it's important to be really stylish when you're in a band? Like, are we supposed to dress up or something?"

She shrugs. "I don't want to dress up. I like being comfortable, don't you? Maybe we'll be known as that cool band with girls who wear awesome sneakers. Nothing wrong with that."

I nod, because she's right. There's a knock at the door, which means Abigail's here. We say hello and head down to the basement. When Mom and Dad bought this house ten years ago, it was the soundproof studio Dad loved the most. And I have to say, it's pretty great knowing that when we shut the door, our noise—I mean, our music—won't bother anyone. Abigail goes to work hooking up her pretty red guitar to the amplifier. My dad's been really nice about letting us use his studio equipment. He has top-of-the-line equipment that he uses for his performances, but the stuff in his studio wasn't cheap either.

He spent an hour or so going over rules with us. Everything basically came down to this one: Do not break anything or you will be grounded for the rest of your life.

"Before we start playing, I really think we should come up with a name," Abigail says, fishing a guitar pick out of her jeans pocket. She's been taking guitar lessons for about six months, and she's getting pretty good.

"I hate coming up with names," I say, thinking about the Baking Bookworms and how my mind went blank and I couldn't even offer any other suggestions. "It's so hard. How do people do it? Where do you think the New Pirates got their name?"

"I don't know," Zola says as she takes a seat behind the drum set. "It's an awesome name, if you ask me."

"What about the Cherry Pickers?" Abigail asks. "I'd love something fun like that."

"Um, I don't like cherries," Zola says. "No offense."

"Maybe we can stay away from food-related names?" I suggest. "They kind of make me nervous. Long story."

"We could go with something like the Zombies or the Ninjas," Zola says. "I'd rather be a ninja than a pirate any day."

Abigail slips the guitar strap around her neck and strums. It's really loud, so she turns the volume down on the amp. "Nah. Too much like the Pirates. I want to be different from them."

I look around the room, trying to think of something that's fun and unique. Something that feels like us. I keep looking at Zola's shoes, wondering if we could do something related to them. The Polka Dots is a cute name, but people would probably expect us to play polka music, and polka is about the last thing I want to play.

The Sneakers?

The Sneaker Dots?

The Dots?

"You guys," I say, "what about something really simple? Like the Dots?"

"Hey, I like it," Zola says. "Do you think it's too simple, though?"

Abigail smiles. "The Dots. No. It's easy to remember, and that's good."

"Yeah, I like it too," I say. "Here, let me try it out. Ladies and gentlemen, for this year's Spring Fling, I'm pleased to introduce to you a band that's as fun as their name—the Dots!"

Abigail and Zola clap and cheer. It makes me laugh.

After we calm down, I say, "So now that our name is settled, do you guys want to compete in the auditions coming up in a few weeks?"

"Yes," they say at the exact same time.

"But shouldn't we perform an original song?" I ask.

Abigail pulls a crumpled piece of paper out of her back pocket. "Well, I've been working on something. We can try it out, if you want to."

"Is it a cupcake song?" I ask.

She shakes her head. "No, it isn't. Lily, you are the one who got us into that mess, so I think you're the one who gets to work on a cupcake song."

Zola looks at us like we are crazy. "Dudes, what are you talking about?"

"Lily promised the New Pirates that if we're chosen to play at the Spring Fling," Abigail explains, "we'll play a cupcake song they'll love."

"Don't forget the dance," I say, cringing. "That was your idea, Abigail."

"Sorry, Lily. If you write the song, I think it makes sense you come up with the dance too," Abigail says.

"So what's the song called you've been working on?" Zola asks.

"'Wishing.' Here, I'll play a little bit for you."

Abigail puts the piece of paper on the music stand in front of her and then strums her guitar and starts to sing.

"I blew on the dandelion, and watched the wishes fly.
Some fell to the ground while others floated high.
Maybe life is hard sometimes, but that's just how it goes.
If we hope and if we wish, life might change, who knows."

She stops playing. "That's all I've got. Sorry. I need to work on the chorus. Maybe you guys can help me?"

"Abigail, that's really good," I say. "If we can finish it and then practice like crazy the next couple of weeks, we might have a chance at winning that audition."

"Can you play it from the top?" Zola asks, which sounds so professional and like we're really a band.

That's when it hits me, and I want to squeal and jump around because I'm in a *real* band and we have a name and we might even have a song!

I'm so excited, but I tell myself to calm down because there is still a lot of work to do. Before we're able to get too far into the song, someone knocks on the studio door. I open the door just enough to peek out and see my mom standing there.

"Sorry to bother you," she says. She's holding a piece of paper with a phone number written on it. "Isabel just called and I thought you might want to call her back before it gets too late. She said it was important, and she didn't have your cell number, so she called the house."

"We're right in the middle of something," I tell her as I take the piece of paper. "I'll have to wait and call her in a little while."

Mom nods. "Well, if you girls want to take a break pretty soon, I bought some peanut-butter cookies at the store. They're really good."

"Okay. Thanks."

I shut the door and go back to the band. Not just any band. My band—the Dots!

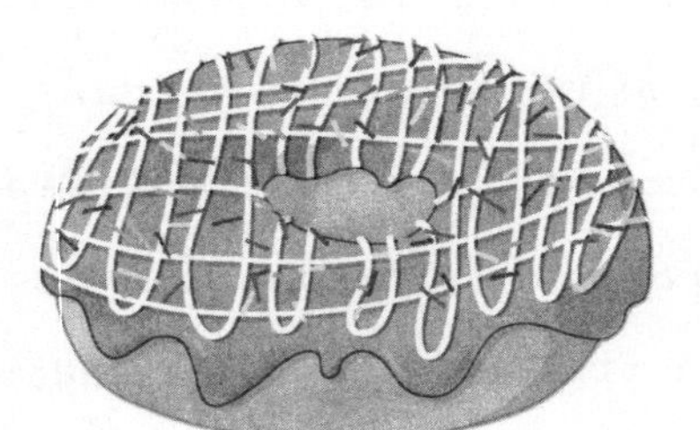

Chapter 5

applesauce cake

GOOD FOR CALMING NERVES

We manage to get some more lyrics written to our song, though it's still not finished. I sing while the girls play the instruments, and we don't sound half-bad. We don't sound great yet either, but that's to be expected with a brand-new song.

I ask the girls if we can take a break, so we go upstairs and Abigail and Zola munch on cookies at the kitchen table while I excuse myself for a minute and take the phone into the living room.

"Isabel?" I say when she answers. "This is Lily."

"Oh, thanks for calling me back. Your mom said your band is practicing tonight. That's so amazing you're in a band. What do you play?"

I take a seat on the sofa. "I don't play an instrument. I'm the lead singer. I should probably learn guitar at some point, but my parents have been paying for voice lessons, and lessons are pretty expensive."

"Yeah. I bet. Hey, the reason I called is because Sophie's thirteenth birthday is coming up in a couple of weeks. I want to have a surprise party for her."

"Oh, wow, I love that idea," I say. "Is there anything I can do to help?"

"Actually, there is. Our apartment isn't very big, so I was hoping you might be willing to have the party at your house. Do you think your mom would mind?"

"Oh, um, I don't think so." I get up and walk toward Mom's office. "Let me ask her right now. When's her birthday?"

"It's March sixteenth, which is a Saturday, lucky

for us. You could have it in the afternoon or evening, whatever you think is best."

"Okay. Can you hold on a second, Isabel?"

"Sure."

I knock lightly on Mom's office door.

"Come in," Mom calls out.

I cover the phone with the palm of my hand and go in. "Mom, Isabel wants to have a surprise party for Sophie. She's turning thirteen in a couple of weeks. Do you think we could have the party here?"

Mom smiles. "Oh, sweetie, I'd love to do that! Sophie has been such a good friend to you. What's the date? I'll check my calendar to make sure we're free."

"March sixteenth."

She clicks on her laptop, studies it for a second, and then says, "Yep. That'll be fine. Oh, how fun! I love surprise parties!"

I step out of her office and shut the door as I put the phone back to my ear. "Isabel? My mom said we could have the party here."

"Perfect! We have a lot we need to talk about and so much to do, but I know you need to get back to your band. We'll need to meet up at least once this week and get invitations made and buy some decorations and figure out food. Do you have time tomorrow?"

I'm thinking fast, trying to figure out how I can make this work. I have an essay for social studies I have to work on after school. "After dinner would probably be best. Where do you want to meet?"

"If your mom can bring you here, we can sit in the cupcake shop and eat cupcakes while we talk about the party."

"Sounds good. I'll be there around seven."

"Great. Thanks, Lily. See you then."

I head back to the kitchen, where Abigail and Zola have finished off the cookies and are entertaining themselves by playing table hockey with a guitar pick.

"Sorry about that," I tell them. "We can head back to the studio now and work on those song lyrics some more."

Zola looks at her phone. "Actually, my dad is on his way to pick me up. He's going to be here any minute. I need to get my sticks from downstairs."

"Should we set up another time to practice?" Abigail asks as she and Zola stand up. "What about tomorrow night?"

"Sorry. I can't," I say. "I have something else I have to do." Now I feel guilty about making plans with Isabel before checking with Abigail and Zola. "What about Wednesday?"

"Wednesday I have guitar lessons," Abigail says.

"And Thursday night I have drum lessons," Zola says.

"Friday?" I ask.

They both nod. "Yeah, that should work," Zola says.

I breathe a sigh of relief. "Okay, good. Friday it is."

"Work on that cupcake song between now and then, okay?" Abigail says with a wink.

"How about if I eat a cupcake instead?" I say, thinking of the cupcake shop where I'll be meeting Isabel tomorrow night.

We hustle down to the studio and collect their things. Both of their parents arrive a few minutes later.

After they leave, I rustle around in the kitchen, looking for something to eat, when Madison comes in.

"How'd band practice go?" she asks.

I turn around as she sets a plastic bag on the counter. "It was fun. What's that?"

"Leftover applesauce cake from the potluck tonight. You can have some if you want. It's pretty good. Mom picked it up at the bakery."

I take the cake out of the bag. "Was the potluck a basketball thing?"

She leans against the counter, and I can't help but notice how strong she looks. Her arms have so much definition to them, and I wonder if she lifts weights on top of everything else she does to stay fit.

"Yeah. End-of-the-season party. I was kind of down about the season ending, but I'm feeling better now."

I cut a piece of cake and put it on a plate. "How come?"

"Some of my friends talked me into going out for softball. Tryouts are this week."

I get a fork out of the silverware drawer. "Softball? But you've never played. Volleyball and basketball have always been your sports."

She shrugs. "I figure it doesn't hurt to try. My friends tell me softball is a blast. And if I make the team, it'll be a good way to keep myself in shape."

"Well, good luck with that," I say as I sit at the table with my piece of cake.

Mom comes out of her office and joins us. "Lily, here's the book for our next book club meeting. I bought two copies for us, so you don't have to worry about rushing through it."

She sets a copy of *The View from Saturday* down in front of me. I feel a tiny knot in the pit of my stomach, because there's one more thing on my growing list of things I have to do in the next few weeks. I take a bite of cake to distract myself from the nervous-making thoughts.

"Mom," I say, "I told Isabel I'd meet up with her at the cupcake shop tomorrow night, to start planning for Sophie's party. Can you drive me there after dinner?"

"Yes," she says as she gets herself a piece of cake. "I'm happy to do that." She looks at Madison. "We're having a surprise party for a friend of Lily's here in a couple of weeks."

Madison nods. "Please remind me a couple of days before the party so I can make sure I have something else to do far, far away that day. I don't want to get sucked into cleaning house or decorating or baking or any of the other hundred things you guys will be doing."

I gulp.

"It probably will be a lot of work," Mom says, "but it'll be worth it. Right, Lily?"

I take another bite of cake, hoping to distract myself again.

What have I gotten myself into?

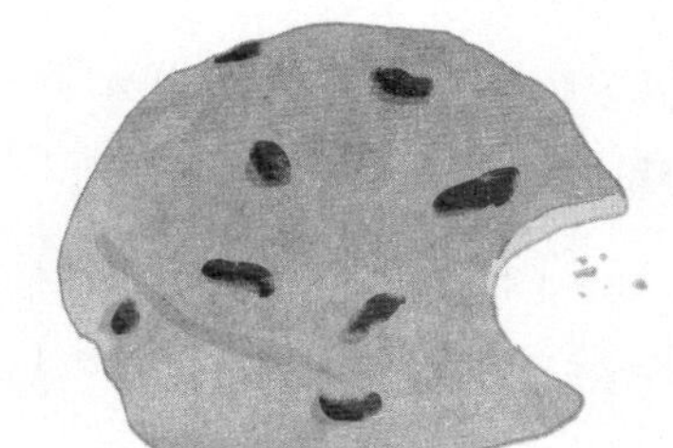

Chapter 6

cookies-'n'-cream cupcakes

FLAVOR OVERLOAD

When I get to It's Raining Cupcakes on Tuesday evening, it's almost dark, but I can see Isabel waiting in front of the brightly lit shop.

"I'm going grocery shopping while you two chat," Mom says. "I'll be back in about an hour."

"Okay," I tell her as I get out of the car. "Thanks, Mom."

She waves and drives off.

"Hi, Isabel," I say.

"Hey, Lily. Thanks for coming." She opens the door to the shop and we step inside. It smells like freshly baked cake. Delicious! Isabel locks the door and says, "We're not actually open right now, but my mom said we could sit at a table and have a cupcake while we talk about the party."

"Where are all the cupcakes?" I ask as I scan the empty cases.

"Oh, we take them out of the cases before we close every afternoon," Isabel explains. "Whatever is left over, we sell the following day at a discount. They're called day-old cupcakes. They still taste good, but we want people to know that the cupcakes in the cases are always really fresh, baked the same day. Follow me. I'll show you."

We go around the cash register and back into the kitchen. She walks over to a big plastic tub on the counter.

"Let's see," she says as she pops the lid off. "You get to choose from cookies 'n' cream, coconut bliss, banana-cream pie, or red velvet. What looks good?"

"They all look fantastic." I try to imagine what each one might taste like. Red velvet is my favorite, but I kind of want to try something different tonight. "I think I'll go with the cookies 'n' cream."

Isabel smiles. "Excellent choice." She grabs a pair of plastic tongs, picks up a cookies-'n'-cream cupcake for me, and places it on a pretty yellow plate. She chooses banana-cream pie for herself.

"You must feel like the luckiest girl in the world," I tell her. "You get to eat cupcakes anytime you want."

"I kind of get sick of them sometimes, to be honest. But my mom loves her cupcake shop, and while business was slow for a while, things have picked up, so that's good. We have Sophie to thank for that. I feel lucky to have Sophie as a best friend, that's for sure."

The way she says it, I feel like I'm watching two friends whisper back and forth, sharing a secret. "What did she do?"

"Once a month or so, she comes and walks around the neighborhood, wearing a cupcake costume she made, to help bring us business. She looks amazing and, at the same time, a little bit ridiculous, but she doesn't care. She's helping us, and that's all that matters to her."

"Wow," I say. In that moment, I'm so jealous of Isabel and the close friendship she has with Sophie, but I try to not let it show. Softly, I say, "You are lucky. What a good friend. She's never said anything about that to me."

Isabel hands me the plates. "That's Sophie for you. She's not the type to brag about herself, right?" She points toward the dining area. "Find the table with the pad of paper and pen, and take a seat. I'll get us some milk."

"Okay, thanks." I go back to the dining area and see the paper she was talking about. I sit down in one of the two chairs, still thinking about what Isabel said. This surprise party is my chance to show Sophie she's one of my best friends. I have to do everything I can to make it a really great party.

I turn the pad of paper toward me and read what Isabel has written.

Things to do for Sophie's party:

1. Make a list of people to invite
2. Make or buy invitations
3. Pass out invitations
4. Buy decorations
5. Plan menu
6. Games or something else fun to do?
7. Come up with a plan to get Sophie to Lily's house
8. Buy gift

"My dad loves lists," Isabel says as she sits down with the glasses of milk. "I guess I take after him."

"Yeah, it's a good way to really see everything that needs to be done," I tell her, secretly panicking inside at all the things that need to be done.

I peel the liner off of my cupcake.

"I've been working on a list of people to invite," Isabel says, flipping the pad to another piece of paper. "I hope thirty isn't too many?"

I almost drop my cupcake. "Thirty?"

"It's really hard to narrow it down any more than that because I don't want anyone to feel left out. And

I think I should invite both boys and girls, because we have some boys who we're good friends with at school. Think your mom will be okay with thirty kids, both boys and girls?"

"Uh, sure."

She smiles. "Oh, good. I was hoping you'd say that. My dad said he'd help me make some invitations on the computer, so I'm going to do that tonight, when we're done here. I should be able to hand them out to everyone tomorrow."

I am giving myself a little pep talk right now. This is what it sounds like in my brain.

It'll be okay, Lily. Think of your algebra class—that's about thirty kids. It's not so many, right? It'll be fun. What does Dad always say? The more the merrier? The important thing is to make Sophie happy. Isabel is going to help you with everything, so it's not like you're going to have that much to do. Look. She's handling all of the invitations, and that's a big job. Remain calm. Eat your cupcake. It will be fine.

I bite into my cupcake and the creamy taste of vanilla frosting mixed with Oreo cookie hits my tongue, and it's really, really good. I take a deep breath and close my eyes for a second, savoring the flavor.

"What time do you want to have the party?" Isabel asks.

And just like that, I'm back from the sweetness of cupcakes to the business of party planning. "Mom and I talked about it on the ride over," I tell her. "Is seven o'clock okay? That way we don't have to worry about serving a meal."

"Perfect," Isabel says, writing down seven o'clock on her pad of paper. "Can you give me your address?"

She hands me the pen and paper, and I write down all of my information, including my cell phone number. While I'm doing that, she says, "I figure I'll get purple and silver decorations. Purple and silver look pretty together, don't you think?"

"Ooooh, that sounds nice."

"I can come to your house early that day and help you decorate. I don't want you to have to do it all alone."

Isabel looks at the list and points to number five. "So, what do you think we should do for food?"

"I wonder if your mom might want to donate some cupcakes," I say. It seems like a good solution to me. And who doesn't like cupcakes?

She taps the pen on the table, thinking about my question. "The thing is, Sophie has cupcakes here all the time. I want something special for her birthday. This is the big thirteen, right? She should have an amazing dessert for becoming a teenager."

I feel my cheeks getting warm. Isabel must think I'm an idiot. I have to show her that I want something amazing for Sophie too. "Right. Of course she should have something really special. I bet I can find a dessert that's out of this world."

"Really?"

I try to sound excited, even though I'm actually terrified as to whether or not I can pull it off. "Sure."

"Awesome," she says, writing my name next to number five on her list. "I know you'll make something fantastic."

When she says the word "make," my stomach lurches. It feels like I'm on a giant roller coaster, heading down, down, down. "Well," I quickly say, "we have this great bakery nearby that my mom goes to . . ." I stop because Isabel looks like I've just told her I want to serve asparagus and mud pies at the party. It's like the mother/daughter book club meeting all over again. She really wants me to make something. I try to save myself from complete embarrassment. "Maybe I can get some ideas there."

"Maybe. I bet your mom would love to help you make something. And what about your older sister? Does she like to bake?"

"Not really. She's into sports."

She nods, like it makes complete sense. "Well, you're one of the Baking Bookworms," she says, taking a bite of her cupcake. When she's done chewing, she smiles. "Which means there isn't a single baking challenge you can't handle, right?"

I should have suggested a different name.

The Bashful Bookworms.

The Babbling Bookworms.

The Brilliant Bookworms.

Why didn't I suggest a different name? And why did I agree to cohost Sophie's birthday party?

Chapter 7

cinnamon rolls

A COMFORTING SNACK

From the time I was three years old, I loved to sing. Mom says I could sing better than I could talk. I get that from my dad. If my dad isn't playing music, he's usually listening to it, and apparently I loved to sing along to whatever song was on the radio, whether I knew all the words or not.

I wish other things came as easily to me. When I was six, Mom signed me up for soccer. It seems like there's always one kid who can't do anything right and runs the wrong way down the field and scores a goal for the other team. I was that kid. I was horrible. My dad tried to tell me it didn't matter, that the most important thing was to have fun. Easy for him to say. I'm pretty sure he'd never scored a point for the opposite team.

When I get home from school on Wednesday, I take out every cookbook we own. All three of them. They look brand-new. Mom probably got them at her bridal shower years ago, stuck them in the cupboard, and hasn't looked at them since. She's a pretty basic cook. Tacos are about as complicated as she gets in the kitchen.

I flip through the cookbook by Betty Crocker and find the dessert section. I don't know what I'm looking for, exactly, other than something that says Sophie and birthday party. I figure I'll know it when I see it.

"Hey, Lily Dilly." Dad strolls over to the fridge and pulls out a bottle of water.

"Hey, Dad."

After he takes a drink, he rummages around

for a minute, until he eventually pulls out a tube of something. "Think I'll make cinnamon rolls. Sounds like a good afternoon snack, right?"

My stomach grumbles at the mention of those two pretty words. It's been a few hours since I ate my peanut-butter-and-honey sandwich for lunch.

"Right."

He hits a couple of buttons on the oven and it starts preheating. Then he pulls a baking pan out of the cupboard, pops the tube open, and places the unbaked cinnamon rolls in a circle on the pan.

Maybe I could do that for Sophie's party. Buy a bunch of tubes of cinnamon rolls from the grocery store, bake them up ahead of time, frost them, and pass them off as homemade. Would anyone even know the difference?

Dad sits down across from me and takes another swig from his water bottle. His cheeks are really pink and his short brown hair is sticking every which way. Either he's been working on a new song for hours and hours or he just got off his treadmill.

He must know I'm trying to figure out why he

looks the way he does because he says, "I went for a four-mile run on the treadmill."

I nod. "I didn't think you got that sweaty playing music."

He smiles. "Not in the studio, no. Playing on a stage with hot lights for two hours, yes."

"Are your shows at the Wallflower going all right?" I ask.

"Oh, yeah. They're great. We've had a good crowd every night." The oven beeps, letting us know it's preheated, so he jumps up and sticks the rolls in. "What about you? How's your band coming along?"

I sigh. "We have half a song written. We're getting together again Friday night. I hope we can finish it. We want to audition for the Spring Fling at school."

He sits down again and raises his eyebrows. "You guys are trying out for a gig? That's awesome, kiddo! You're going big-time." He raises his hand and we high-five. "Just remember what I told you. Make the music your priority. All the rest will work out if you focus on making great music."

I nod. "I'm supposed to write a cupcake song. A

sophisticated cupcake song. Think you can help me with that?"

He points to the cookbooks in front of me. "Is that what you're doing? Looking for a little inspiration in those books?"

"No. The cookbooks are because I'm supposed to make a fabulous dessert for thirty people at a surprise birthday party in a week and a half."

He laughs and leans back in his chair. "Hold on a second. What are you doing to yourself, Lily? That's an awful lot you've got on your plate."

I shake my head. "Believe me. I know."

"Can't you just buy a dessert for the party?" he asks. "That's what I'd do. I'm happy to give you some money to shop at Mom's favorite bakery. Or what if we get a whole bunch of brownies from Beatrice's Brownies?"

I laugh. "Dad, the party is for Sophie. She's the girl who's done television commercials for Beatrice's Brownies. She's probably sick of those things by now."

"Well, what's wrong with a huge bakery cake, then? I know. We can have it decorated like that musical you saw with Sophie a few months back. What was it called?"

"*Wicked*," I tell him. "And I'm not really sure a cake with the Wicked Witch of the West's face in green frosting would be very appetizing."

"Hmm," he says. "You may be right. Well, think it over. I'm happy to help however I can. Though if you're going to try and make something yourself, I'm probably not your guy. Wait. That reminds me. There's a chef on TV I was watching last Sunday when I was fiddling around on my guitar. Have you ever seen the show *Secrets of a Pastry Chef*?"

I close the cookbook because all it's doing is making me even more hungry. The cinnamon rolls are starting to smell really good. "I scheduled the DVR to record it. I think it only shows on Sundays."

"You should double-check," he says. "They might be playing reruns on other days of the week. Chef Smiley takes you through all of the steps of a recipe, and he makes it look so easy. I'm telling you, Lily, he might be the answer to your baking problems."

"Okay. I'll see what I can find."

He stands up and walks over to the oven. "As far

as the cupcake song, I'll let you know if any lyrics or a fun melody come to mind."

The timer goes off. The cinnamon rolls are done. I wish I could just pop a few notes in the oven and have a complete song come out. Someone needs to invent that—a song-writing oven.

But knowing me, I'd probably mess that up too.

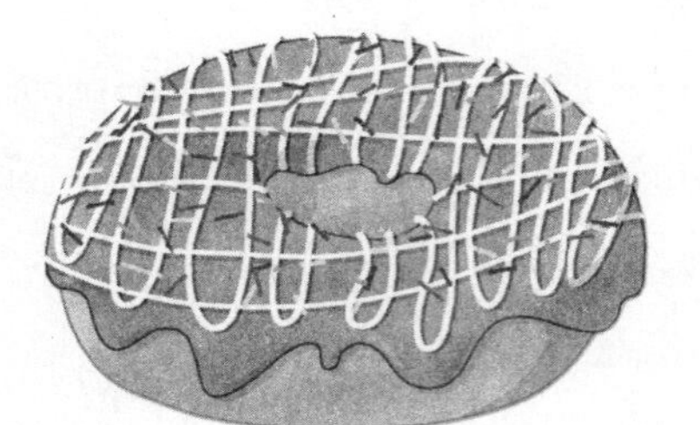

Chapter 8

strawberry cake

PRETTY ENOUGH TO WEAR

Dad was right. They do play reruns of Chef Smiley's show on the Food Channel. After dinner, I settle in on the sofa with a notebook and our kitty, Oscar, to watch an episode. The funny chef takes us start to finish through a strawberry cake made from scratch. The secret ingredient is strawberry-flavored gelatin.

"I know it sounds strange," Chef Smiley says as he

pours the red powdery stuff into the bowl, "but it gives the cake a delicious strawberry flavor. Remember, it isn't always about being fancy and using expensive or exotic ingredients. It's about finding what works. In fact, that's one of my mottos in the kitchen—whatever works!"

I write everything down while Chef Smiley shows us, step by step, how to make the cake. It really doesn't look too hard, and I'm getting more and more excited as the show winds down. When he takes a bite of the cake, he says, "Sweet Uncle Pete, that's good," just like he did last time. I wonder if he has an uncle Pete who's really sweet.

When I'm finished watching, I give the cat one last pet and then go looking for my mom. I find her in the kitchen, unloading the dishwasher. "Good," she says. "I could use an extra set of hands. Can you help me, please?"

I set my notebook down and grab a couple of glasses from the top rack. "Mom, I need a few things from the store so I can make a strawberry cake. Can you take me?"

"Oh, honey, I can't. I need to get a house listed

on the computer tonight. Maybe your sister can take you. Unless it can wait until tomorrow?"

I sigh. "No. I don't want to wait. I have to find something amazing to make for Sophie's party. This strawberry cake may be the answer. It looks so good. And pretty."

She goes to work putting the silverware away. "When we're done here, we'll go find your sister and I'll ask her to drive you."

Madison won't like it, but I know she'll do it. When Madison got the used Ford Escort that Mom and Dad helped pay for, they told her she had a responsibility to help out with errands when necessary.

After we've finished, we head upstairs to Madison's room. Mom knocks. Music is playing. Loudly. She knocks again.

"Come in," Madison calls out. The music gets quieter.

Mom opens the door and we peer inside. Madison is sitting at her desk. Dirty clothes are scattered across the floor and all over her bed. On her nightstand are a whole bunch of dirty dishes.

"Madison, I need you to take your sister to the store, please."

"But, Mom, I'm—"

"Please don't argue. I need you to get up and take her right now. It'll only take a few minutes and then you can get back to whatever it is you're working on. And when you're done with that, you get to clean your room. For goodness' sake, Madison. It smells like a cat died in here."

Madison scrunches up her nose. "Gross. No, it doesn't."

I nod my head. "Yes, it does. I'd start digging around for Oscar if I hadn't just seen him in the family room. It really does stink."

Madison stands up. "Okay, okay, so I've been super busy and haven't had time to clean." She looks at me. "Give me a minute to change out of these shorts. I'll meet you downstairs."

"Thank you, honey," Mom says.

Five minutes later, we're in the car, on our way to the store. "What are you up to?" Madison asks me.

"Isabel expects me to make the dessert for

Sophie's party," I tell her. "So I want to try and make this strawberry cake I just saw on TV. It doesn't look *too* hard."

She shakes her head. "Lily, maybe you should tell your book club friends you're not a baker. I bet they'd understand."

"But maybe I am a baker," I say. "Maybe I just haven't practiced enough. You know what Dad says. Practice makes—"

"Perfect? Look, you know I'm a big believer in practicing myself. But here's the thing—sometimes there are things we just aren't good at doing. I mean, what if I told you I wanted to be a ballerina? Would you tell me if I practice enough, I'll be good enough to perform the *Nutcracker* come Christmastime?"

I look out my window and watch raindrops skip across the glass. "Maybe," I say quietly. "I mean, who knows? Anything is possible, isn't it? Mom and Dad have told us that our whole lives. Are you saying you don't believe it?"

Madison pulls into the Safeway parking lot and parks the car. After she turns the motor off, she looks at me. "Lily, that's what parents are supposed to say. It's okay if you're good at some things and not so good at others. I mean, look around. Who's good at everything?"

I think for a few seconds, and only one person pops into my head, though I'm sure there must be plenty of people. "You?" I say to my sister.

She laughs. "Oh, that is funny. Do you really think I'm good at everything? Come on. Don't you remember how I sing? What'd you say I sounded like last time I tried to sing with you?"

"A seal with the flu."

"Right. And what about my decorating skills? Or my cleaning skills? You saw my room—nothing to brag about there."

I grab my purse and start to get out. "Okay, okay, maybe you're right. But I want to feel like I fit in with the Baking Bookworms. I like those girls, and I want them to like me. I want to be good at baking, Madison. So I'm going to see if Chef Smiley can teach me. It doesn't hurt to try."

"All right. Hurry up and buy what you need," she says as I get out. "I have a paper to write and a room to clean, thanks to you, Miss Baker-Wannabe."

I grab a grocery cart and make my way through the store, crossing things off my list. The recipe calls for sifted flour, and I remember what Chef Smiley said. *With the right tools and the right attitude, baking is a piece of cake.* I throw a flour sifter in my cart, because I'm pretty sure we don't have one at home.

I buy the stuff with the money Mom gave me and hurry back to the car. Madison gives me a hard time about taking forever, but geez, I had to make sure I got everything on my list.

When we get home, Madison retreats to her room and I go to work making the cake. I cream the butter, sugar, and gelatin together with the mixer, just like Chef Smiley said to do. Then I separate the eggs and add the yolks, followed by the whipped egg whites. I mix the flour and baking powder together, and stir that in with the milk. I add the vanilla, and the only thing left to do is puree the frozen strawberries.

I get the blender out, put a bunch of strawberries in along with some water, and hit blend.

"Lily!" Mom yells behind me. "You don't have the . . ."

But it's too late. Bright red strawberries go everywhere—on the counter, the cupboards, the floor, the ceiling, and yes, some get on me too.

I push the off button and turn around to face my mother.

"Oh, honey," she says, trying not to laugh, which I guess is better than yelling at me. "Always make sure to put the lid on the blender."

I am so embarrassed. And everything was going so well. "Yeah, I think I know that now."

I look down at my white shirt, dots of strawberry juice all over it. It's probably ruined.

"Why don't you go change your clothes?" Mom says. "I'll start cleaning up in here."

"But what about the cake? I'm almost done with the batter. I just need to add the pureed strawberries and bake it."

"Do you have any berries left?"

Thankfully, I'd dumped only half of the big bag into the blender. "Yes. They're in the freezer. Can I finish really quickly and then go shower?"

"All right," she says, wetting a rag in the sink. "I'll work around you."

I blend more strawberries, this time keeping everything inside the blender. I pour them into the batter and mix it well. Then I put the parchment paper in the bottom of the pans, just like Chef Smiley instructed. He said it keeps the cakes from sticking. He also said the batter makes enough for three pans, but we have only two, so I split the batter between the two pans. After I pop them in the oven, I set the timer and thank Mom for helping to clean up.

"You're welcome," she says. "Come and help me when you're finished, okay?"

"I think I might take a shower. If I'm not down in twenty-five minutes, can you check the cakes? Check them with a toothpick. It should come out clean."

"Okay," she says, grabbing a stool so she can get to the ceiling.

"I'm really sorry, Mom," I tell her again. "Hopefully, the cake will taste delicious and you can have a big piece."

She holds up her hand with her fingers crossed. "That's what I'm hoping for!"

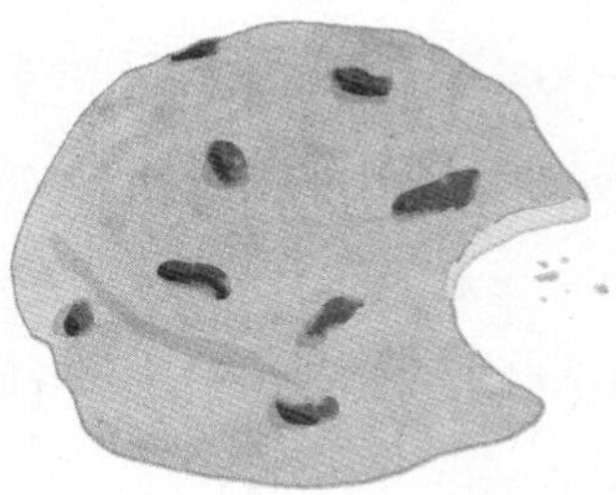

Chapter 9

glazed doughnuts

A TRUE JOY

I'm heading to choir, and I'm so tired, I could probably lie down in the hallway and take a nap. Okay, maybe not. After all, the hallway is where hundreds of kids walk and it wouldn't be very nice to take a nap where I'd be trampled. Not to mention the fact that I'd be sleeping in dirt.

But I am *so* tired.

Last night, after I took a shower and dried my

hair, I went downstairs and smelled something bad. Mom was nowhere in sight. The timer was beeping and the cakes were done. They weren't burnt, but the oven was filled with smoke because I guess I filled the cake pans too full. The bottom of the oven was covered with burnt batter that had dripped from the pans as the cake rose.

My mother had stepped away to take a call. When my mom gets on the phone, the sky could be falling and she wouldn't notice.

After I opened the windows to clear out the smoke, I considered my options. I could call the whole thing a disaster and throw out the cakes. Or I could frost the cakes even though they weren't perfect and see how they tasted, and then decide if I wanted to attempt it all over again for Sophie's party.

I decided I wanted to see my recipe through to the end. I'd already put in a lot of work, plus I was curious how the cake would taste. Mom came back a while later and felt really bad. While she frosted the cake, I finished wiping down the kitchen.

The cake was not pretty, due to the layers being uneven. When I took a bite, I thought for sure it would taste as bad as it looked. What a surprise when it turned out to be delicious! Mom and I were still up when Dad got home, and he thought it tasted good too.

Now I'm trying to decide if I want to try again on Sophie's big day, or look for a different recipe. Maybe something a little easier. I figure I'd have to make two cakes in order to feed thirty people, which means I'd have twice the chances of messing up.

"Hey, Lily," Belinda says as I enter the choir room. She never really talks to me. Weird.

"Hey," I say. "How's it going?"

"Fine." She smiles. "How's the audition practicing going?"

I try to sound happy. Confident. "Oh, it's going really well."

She narrows her eyes. "Really? That's great. Are you guys going to audition with your cupcake song?"

I cross my arms. "Oh no. We want to save that song for the Spring Fling. Because it's . . . special, you know?"

She smirks. "Right. I'm sure it is."

"What about you guys? Have you decided what

song you're going to play in the audition?"

She casually picks at one of her fingernails. "No, not yet. We have over thirty songs to choose from, so it's not easy. We want to perform one that shows our experience and our depth as musicians." She looks at me. "We *really* want to win."

I gulp. Thirty songs? Depth as musicians? What does that even mean? I'm not sure how to reply and lucky for me, the bell rings, so I don't have to.

We start to move toward the risers, where we'll take our places, but Mr. Weisenheimer calls out, "Kids, I brought doughnuts for you today. Come over and get one and take a seat in the chairs. I want to talk to you for a few minutes before we start singing."

I make my way toward the table with the boxes of doughnuts. Everyone is smiling and laughing and thanking Mr. Weisenheimer for bringing us an unexpected treat.

After we're all seated and munching away, he stands in front of us and smiles. "Wow. What a bunch of happy kids. Wish I could bring doughnuts for you every day."

"You should!" someone from the back calls out.

Everyone laughs.

"You all know that I think you did an amazing job at the winter concert. And I've talked about how I want the spring concert in May to be even better. And while we've worked hard on the technical aspects, like breathing, pitch, and tone, I haven't spent any time talking about what I believe to be most important when it comes to singing. Does anyone want to take a guess as to what I think is most important?"

No one answers.

He walks over to the dry-erase board on the wall and writes the word "Joy."

"I want to talk to you about singing with feeling and pulling on the heart strings of the people listening to you. Just like you're eating those doughnuts with joy, I want you to sing with joy. To feel the music with your entire body and to let your audience in on what you're feeling." He pauses and looks at us. "Yes, you have to have a certain amount of talent to go far as a singer. But I truly believe that talent will only get you so far. The people who go to the top are the people who sing because they love it more than anything else. And it shows."

Belinda raises her hand. "I disagree."

Our teacher nods and smiles. "Okay. How come?"

"Without talent," Belinda says, "and I'm talking true talent, you're nothing. You'll get nowhere."

"You may be right," Mr. Weisenheimer says. "But my point is, be excited about what you're doing. Don't just go through the motions. When you're singing, feel the song and let the audience see and hear and feel those emotions as well. Understand?"

I think I understand, so I nod my head, along with most everyone else.

"All right," he says. "Then let's do what we love to do, shall we? Let's sing!"

After school, Isabel calls me. I'm sitting at the kitchen table, looking through the cookbooks again, eating an apple.

"I just wanted to check in with you," she says, "and let you know the invitations are all passed out. I'm already starting to get replies from people about whether or not they can come. I'll try to have a final count to you by Monday or Tuesday. Is that okay?"

"Sure," I say. "That'll be fine."

"Have you decided what you're going to bake for the big day?"

I laugh nervously. "Not yet. I'm trying out some recipes, hoping to find something really wonderful."

"You know," Isabel says, "I was thinking that it should be something chocolate. Sophie loves chocolate. She even loves chocolate chips in her pancakes."

When I slept over at Sophie's house one time, we had chocolate-chip pancakes for breakfast. Isabel's right. The dessert needs to be chocolate. That means the strawberry cake is definitely out. I think of the white-chocolate raspberry cheesecake recipe Chef Smiley is supposed to talk about on Sunday. "Do you think white chocolate is okay?" I ask.

"Yeah. I think so. I mean, chocolate is chocolate, right?" In my mind it is. Isabel continues. "I'm going to buy the decorations this weekend. We still need to come up with a plan to get Sophie to your house. So let's think about that. Maybe you can call her and invite her over there to do something. I don't know. But we need to come up with an idea soon, so Sophie doesn't make other plans for that night."

I tell her I'll brainstorm ideas and we agree to talk again on Monday.

After we hang up, I give myself a pep talk because I want to believe everything is going to turn out fine. Maybe even better than fine. I'll find a delicious chocolate dessert and Sophie is going to come to my house and be totally surprised. She'll be so impressed with everything I did for her, our friendship will be just as strong as the one she has with Isabel.

Here's the thing about pep talks given by yourself and to yourself. It's too easy to roll your eyes and say, "What do you know, anyway?"

Chapter 10

cocoa fudge cake

MUSIC TO A CHOCOHOLIC'S EAR

After dinner Friday night, while Mom goes to watch Dad's last night at the Wallflower, I decide to bake a chocolate cake from a recipe I found in one of our three cookbooks. Mom said it would be okay, since Madison is home, but she made me promise not to burn the house down.

Obviously, my mom has a lot of confidence in my baking skills.

I have about thirty minutes before Zola and Abigail will arrive for practice. I figure it's enough time to get the cake batter mixed up, and then it can bake while we're practicing.

The recipe is called cocoa fudge cake, probably because cocoa is one of the ingredients. I love hot cocoa as a drink, so I figure I'll love the cake too. After I put on an apron, I pull out the flour, sugar, the can of hot cocoa powder, baking soda, salt, and shortening from the pantry. I get the eggs and milk from the refrigerator and the vanilla from the cupboard where we keep the spices.

I measure the ingredients out one by one and put everything in a large mixing bowl. I've just added the last ingredient, the teaspoon of vanilla, when the doorbell rings.

Both Zola and Abigail are standing on the porch when I open the door.

"Hey. Cute apron," Abigail says as the girls step inside.

"Thanks." I look down at the apron I'm wearing. It's yellow and pink with little daisies all over it. I'm pretty sure this is the first time it's been worn. After all, my mom doesn't need to wear an apron to drive to the bakery.

"What are you baking?" Zola asks as I lead them into the kitchen.

"A cocoa fudge cake," I say as I stick the beaters into the mixer. "I'm having a birthday party for a friend from theater camp here next Saturday, and I'm trying to figure out what dessert to serve. As soon as I get the cake in the oven, we can go downstairs."

Zola looks behind me. "Dude, it doesn't look like your oven is preheating. My grandma, the best cake maker on the planet, says you always have to preheat the oven."

I set the mixer down and turn around. "Thanks. You're right. I forgot." Once the oven is turned on, I go back to the ingredients. The recipe says to beat on low speed for thirty seconds and then on high speed for three minutes after that. I don't have a watch, so I eye the clock on the microwave as I mix.

When I'm done, I start to walk toward the sink, holding the dirty beaters, when Abigail asks, "Hold on, Lily. Aren't you going to lick the beaters? That's the best part of making a cake."

I run my finger up the side of one of them and taste the batter before I hand both of them off to my friends.

"Wow," I say. "It's really sweet. Do you think it's supposed to be that sweet?"

Zola and Abigail both taste the batter and eye me suspiciously. "How much sugar did you add?" Zola asks.

"One and a half cups, just like it says. I was really careful with every single ingredient. I want this cake to turn out, you guys. Actually, I *need* this cake to turn out."

Abigail shrugs. "It's probably fine. I mean, it's not horrible. When it bakes up, I bet it'll taste good. I haven't ever tried a chocolate cake made from scratch. It's probably supposed to be really sweet. Right?"

Zola doesn't say anything as she takes the beater from Abigail and tosses both of them in the sink. She has her drumsticks stuck in the back pocket of her jeans. She looks so awesome, with her hair in adorable cornrows. And she's wearing her polka-dot shoes again. It's like you can tell she's in a band just by looking at her. I look down at myself, with the cute apron, and realize I look nothing like a person in a band.

"All right. Get that cake in the oven so we can go make some music," Zola says when she turns around. I pour the batter into the cake pans and slide them into the oven just as the oven beeps that it's done preheating.

I set the timer for thirty minutes before we head downstairs.

"Belinda told me the New Pirates have thirty songs written," I tell the girls when we get to Dad's studio. "Can you believe that? We barely have one."

"A half a song," Abigail says as she passes out music for each of us. "That's what we have."

"Just remember," Zola says with a smile, "all we need is one. One amazing song, one amazing performance, and we're in. So let's focus on that. You ready, Dots? From the top!"

I sing while they play, and when we get to the end of what we have written, we brainstorm some more lyrics. Actually, Zola and Abigail brainstorm some more lyrics. I'm too busy watching the clock on the wall to make sure I don't let the cake burn.

"Earth to Lily, Earth to Lily," Abigail says as she brushes the bangs out of her eyes. "Can you help us out here? Please? This is really important. If we don't finish writing the song, we can't practice the song."

"And if we can't practice the song," Zola says, "we can't win the audition. Guaranteed."

Fifteen minutes. That's how long I have before I need to check on the cake. I grab a pencil from Dad's small desk in the corner. "Okay, sorry. I'll focus. How about this? Let's all think quietly on our own for, like, five minutes, and then we'll share and decide which sounds the best. Okay?"

I get two more pencils and pass them to Abigail and Zola. I read over the chorus again and hum the tune in my head.

Wishes swirl and
wishes twirl,
around and around they spin.
Wishes here and
wishes there,
when one comes true, I win.
Wish on stars or

wish with coins,

who cares, all right, just wish!

When you wish, my wish for you

is that your wish comes true.

I wish for my cake to turn out. I wish for it to taste delicious. I wish for the birthday party to be so much fun that Sophie will never forget it. I wish to be remembered forever as the nicest friend in Willow, Oregon, and the best cake baker too.

And so it goes, wish after wish, until Zola says, "Okay. Time's up. Let's share what we have."

I look down at my blank piece of paper. Did I really just spend practically the entire time wishing? Oh brother.

Abigail shares her lyrics, which sound great, and then Zola shares hers, which are good, but not quite as good as Abigail's. When it's my turn, I say, "I really love Abigail's lyrics. I mean, I like yours too, Zola, but can we just go with Abigail's? Mine are pretty terrible, honestly."

"I didn't see you writing anything down," Zola says, her arms crossed as she sits on the stool behind the drums.

I bite my lip, trying to think of how to respond. "Oh, right, well, they're in my head. But I knew they were bad, so I didn't even bother writing them down."

Abigail shrugs. "Okay, let's add my lyrics to the song and we can try them out. See how it sounds." She looks at Zola. "Is that all right with you?"

"I guess so. Seems like this song is going to be Abigail's song, not the Dots' song, but if that's the way you guys want to roll, whatever."

Abigail looks hurt. "Zola, please don't be upset," she says. "Please? You want to write the last verse all by yourself? If you want to do that, it's fine with me. I don't care. Really."

"Maybe we should make Lily write it," Zola says. "Make sure she's committed to this band."

I look at the clock for the fiftieth time tonight and then jump out of my chair. "You guys, I'm sorry, but I have to check on the cake. I'll be right back. I promise. And of course I'm committed to the band. Not everyone can be good at songwriting, okay? I think there are lots of bands where one person mostly writes the songs. It's a special talent, and obviously, Abigail has that talent."

Neither of them says a word, and Zola still looks kind of mad, but I don't have time to try and smooth things over right now. I run out the door and up the stairs. I find Madison at the oven, peeking in on the cake.

"I could smell the chocolate all the way in my room," Madison says. She shuts the oven door and turns around. Her eyebrows are scrunched up and I can tell something's wrong before she even says it. "Something doesn't look right, Lily. They're about done baking, but the cakes didn't rise very much. I don't know what happened, but I think you did something wrong."

The story of my baking life.

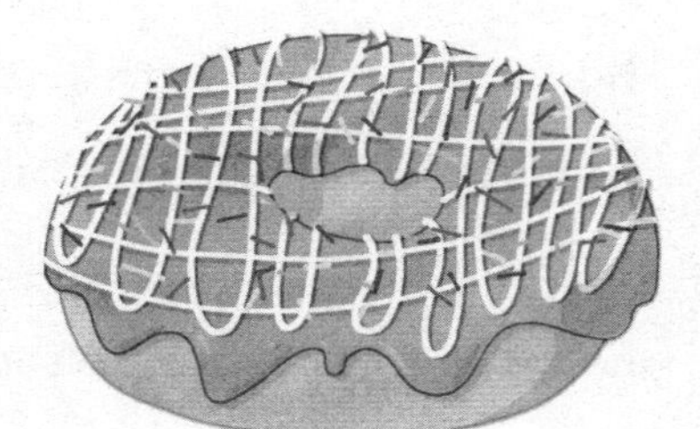

Chapter 11

chocolate marshmallow cookies

PERFECT TO SHARE WITH A FRIEND

After we pulled the pans out of the oven, with the very flat cakes inside of them, I wanted to cry. Madison tried to make me feel better by telling me the cake still might taste good, but it was no use. I felt like a failure.

Abigail and Zola came upstairs a little while later to see why I hadn't come back, their faces telling me they weren't too happy with me. I tried to apologize and offered to go back downstairs with them to practice a while longer, but they just wanted to go home. Madison offered to give them a ride home, so they took off and left me alone with the pathetic cakes. I almost threw them out, but I was curious how they tasted, so I sat there and stared at them, waiting for them to cool off.

Later that night, when my mom got home, she went over the recipe with me. I learned regular milk shouldn't be substituted for buttermilk. Apparently, the buttermilk has an ingredient in it that works with the baking soda to make the cake rise.

That's not the only thing I did wrong, though. When we tried the cake, it tasted terrible. My mom asked what kind of cocoa I used and when I told her about the hot cocoa mix, she explained that when a recipe calls for cocoa, it means unsweetened baking cocoa.

No wonder cake mixes are so popular. Baking a cake from scratch is hard! Like, harder than singing the national anthem at the Super Bowl. Not that I've ever sung the national anthem at the Super Bowl, but still, I can imagine.

Now it's Saturday morning, and I'm trying to figure out what to do next. Mom said she would take me to the store to get the ingredients to try making the cake again, but I don't know if I even want to have the party now.

Actually, I want to have the party and give Sophie a thirteenth birthday she'll never forget, but I don't think I'm good enough to pull it off. What will she think of me if the party turns out to be a disaster just like every recipe I try to make? I want to be someone Sophie admires, not someone she's ashamed of.

I'm trying to get up the nerve to call Isabel, to tell her I can't do it. I stare at the phone, trying to find the right words, when it rings.

"Hello?"

"Hey, Lily. It's Sophie! How are you?"

"Oh, hi, Sophie. I'm all right. What's up?"

"My mom needs to do some shopping for Hayden. He's had a growth spurt and all of his pants are way too short. Every time I see him with his high-water pants and his white socks showing, I can't help but laugh. I guess my mom finally got the hint and figured out she needs to buy him some new ones.

"Anyway, we're going to the mall this afternoon. Thought I'd see if you might want to go with us. We don't have to hang out with them, of course. I want to shop for some new shoes. You know how I love shoes!"

I smile. She does love shoes. I do too. But I should call Isabel. I should practice the audition song. I should write a cupcake song. I should start reading the book for the next book club meeting. I should do a lot of things. But going to the mall for the afternoon sounds like fun and I'm tired of worrying about everything in my life right now.

"Sure. I'd love to go with you."

"Okay," Sophie says. "We'll pick you up around one o'clock. See you then."

"Bye."

Mom tells me she thinks it's a good idea for me to get out of the house and take a break from worrying about the party and everything else. So I eat lunch and get myself ready, and with each passing minute, I'm feeling happier and happier. Sophie and I haven't hung out together in a while and I'm so excited to see her and to do something that doesn't involve flour, sugar, and eggs.

When we get to the mall, Sophie's mom and little brother head in one direction, while Sophie and I take off in another. I have thirty dollars from my allowance that I've saved up, and my mom gave me twenty more, in case I find something special to buy.

We walk toward the big department store, and before we know it, we are laughing our heads off.

First, there's the kiosk in the middle of the mall with the special hand cream called Marvel a salesperson wants us to try. When we say, "No thanks," and keep walking, she walks along with us, begging us to stop and try it.

Then there's the remote-control flying helicopter toy I almost run into, and Sophie can't stop giving me a hard time about it. I was busy making sure the hand cream lady had stopped chasing us down, so I didn't notice the small helicopter flying in the air.

When we finally make it to the shoe department, we collapse into two chairs, trying to keep the laughing tears back.

"I can see it now," Sophie says between her laughs. "The headline reads, 'Girl at mall is seriously injured when she collides with a toy helicopter because she was too busy running from the crazy hand cream lady.'"

"Can I help you?" a man asks us. He's about my dad's age and dressed in a nice, silvery gray suit, with a white shirt and a purple tie.

We stop laughing, because I think that's his way of telling us to behave, in the nicest way possible.

"Look, Sophie," I say, trying to catch my breath, pointing at his tie. "Purple. Your favorite color."

"Or purplicious, as Isabel and I like to say." As I learn of yet another special thing Isabel and Sophie have between them, it feels like someone pokes my heart with a needle. I tell myself it's just a silly word and to forget about it. "I've never seen a purple tie before," Sophie continues. "It goes really well with your silver suit."

"Hey, silver and purple, just like the colors for the . . ." I stop, my hand flying up to my mouth. I can't believe I almost gave it away. I almost told her about the surprise party we've been planning for her. The man must see that I could use some help about now.

"Thank you," he says as he runs his fingers down the side of the tie. "I'm glad you like it. It's one of my favorites. My wife and two sons gave it to me for Father's Day last year. She wasn't sure I'd wear it, but I think it's awesome."

Sophie looks at me. "What were you going to say?"

I'm thankful the guy gave me a minute to think of a good cover. "Oh, um, just that my mom told me when she and my dad got married, their wedding colors were silver and purple."

"That must have been so pretty," she says. "Maybe I'll have those colors at my wedding."

The salesman is still standing there. "We're going to look around," I tell him. "If that's okay."

He nods and smiles. "Absolutely. Just let me know if there's a shoe you'd like to try."

"We will," Sophie says.

Between the two of us, we must try on twenty pairs of shoes. I'm pretty sure the man with the purple tie regrets ever approaching us in the first place. Sophie ends up with a cute pair of wedge sandals, and I buy a pair of polka-dot sneakers, like Zola's, except black with off-white dots. I love them. As I pay for the shoes at the register, I realize I need to call both Abigail and Zola and apologize again for getting distracted last night. Our song isn't finished and it's all my fault. I hope they'll forgive me.

We have some time before we're supposed to meet up with Sophie's mom and brother, so Sophie and I get two giant cookies and two cartons of milk from the Cookie Shack and sit down at a table.

"Yum," Sophie says as she takes a bite of the chocolate marshmallow cookie. "This cookie reminds me of the piece of pie Isabel and I had at Penny's Pie Place. It was the pie Jack made for the baking contest. That's where Isabel met him." We both take a bite at the same time. "Good, huh?"

I nod as I wonder if there's anything that doesn't remind Sophie of Isabel. I start to say something about it and stop myself. That won't do any good. If I want to be as good of a friend to Sophie as Isabel, I have to show her how much she means to me. I realize that one of the best things I can do to make our friendship stronger is to be the person who gives her an amazing birthday party.

She takes another bite of her cookie and I decide to pick her brain while I have the chance. "So if you had to pick one dessert, and that's the only dessert you could eat for the rest of your life, what would it be?"

She sets her cookie down on the plate and wipes her mouth with her napkin. "Well, definitely not brownies. I like them, but after doing the commercials for Beatrice's Brownies, I'm a little tired of them."

"Are you done with those commercials for a while?" I ask as I pick up my carton of milk.

"Yep. All done. My agent is looking for new opportunities for me now."

"Okay," I say, "so no brownies. What would it be, then?"

She leans back in her chair and stares at her plate. "One dessert. And only one. Hm. I guess I'd have to go with the classic chocolate-chip cookie. I mean, no one ever gets tired of chocolate-chip cookies, right?"

"Really? You wouldn't want something more special? More . . . complicated?"

She gives me a funny look. "Complicated? I don't think something has to be complicated to taste good. Sometimes the best things in life are the simplest things, you know?" She smiles. "Like shoe shopping with a friend. Or reading a good book. Which reminds me, have you started the next book yet?"

"No," I say. "I've been so busy with school and my band. Hopefully soon."

"I love the name we came up with for the book club, don't you? The Baking Bookworms. I think it's great we all love to bake."

Just hearing her say that makes my stomach hurt. After all of my recent disasters in the kitchen, I would be thrilled if I never had to turn the oven on again.

I wonder what she'd say if I told her. What would she say if I told her that I wish I could bake as well as she and Isabel do, but baking and I don't seem to get along? Would they kick me out of the book club? I'd hate that. I want to be in the club. More than that, I want to be Sophie's other best friend.

"What about you?" she asks.

I gulp. "What do you mean?"

"If you could only eat one dessert for the rest of your life, what would it be?"

"Oh." I think for a few seconds. "Probably doughnuts. I love doughnuts."

She smiles. "See? You like simple too."

As we eat our cookies, I think about that. Would Isabel be disappointed if I decided to serve something simple, like cookies or doughnuts, at the party? What was it that she said? *She should have an amazing dessert for becoming a teenager.*

Suddenly, making both Isabel and Sophie happy seems about as impossible as beating the New Pirates at the Spring Fling audition.

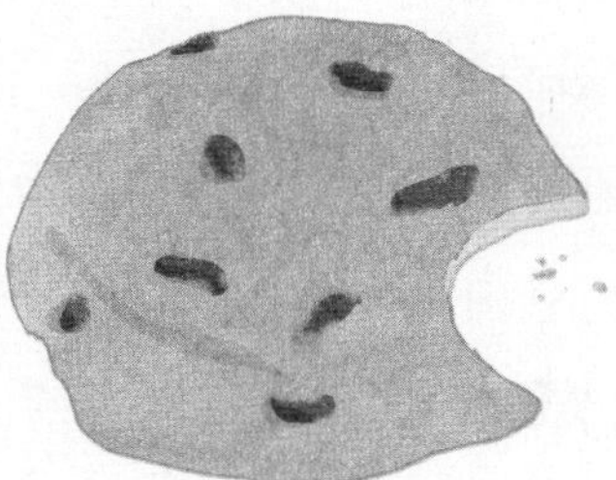

Chapter 12

white-chocolate raspberry cheesecake

A TRUE BAKER'S DELIGHT

It's Sunday night and I'm watching Chef Smiley make cheesecake. And so far I've learned one thing. Sweet Uncle Pete, that's complicated! Yeah, nothing simple about cheesecake, that's for sure.

When I'm done watching, I go find Mom in her office. Her door is open, so I walk in and sit on one of the chairs she has in front of her desk.

"Hi, Lily," she says, not even looking up from her computer. "How's it going?"

"Not so good."

Now she looks up. "How come?"

"Tomorrow Isabel wants me to tell her what I've decided to do as far as food goes for Sophie's birthday party, and I have absolutely no idea."

Now she stops what she's doing and looks at me. "Honey, if it were up to you, and it didn't matter what anyone else thought, what would you serve at the party?"

"I don't know. I've been trying to think of something fun and different. Something . . . special. But not too hard. That's the problem. Everything I might like to make just seems too complicated."

Mom types something into her computer. "You know what I think we could make fairly easily? And would be really fun and unique? I saw some at the coffee shop earlier today."

"What?"

"Cake pops. Have you heard of those? They're little pieces of frosted cake on a stick. Here, I found a how-to video. Come watch."

I hop up and go stand behind her. The lady in the video walks us through how to make them. You bake a cake using a mix in a rectangle pan, let it cool, and then you break up the cake into pieces in a big mixing bowl. You add some canned frosting to the bowl (that helps the cake stick together), mix again, and roll the mixture into small balls. They go in the freezer for a few hours before they're dipped in icing made by melting chocolate coating pieces, either white or regular chocolate. You put lollipop sticks into the balls, dip them in the icing, and finally, roll them in decorations.

"Mom, those are so cute!" I say. "And because you crumble the cake up after it's baked, it doesn't matter if it comes out of the oven crooked or lumpy or a hundred other things."

Mom smiles. "Exactly. And we could use a cake mix from the store. I think together you and I could make these cake pops."

"You really think so?" I ask her.

She stands up and pulls me into a hug. "Yes. I do. I'm pretty sure it'll be a piece of cake."

I smile at her joke, even though I've heard it

before from Chef Smiley, as I pull away. "Should we practice first?"

"Lily, I have a really busy week. And I know you have other things you should be doing too. Let's wait and deal with them on Saturday. We'll make them work. I promise. Is there anything else you'd like to serve?"

"Maybe some chocolate-chip cookies? They're Sophie's favorite."

She nods. "How about if we get some cookie dough at the store? That way all you have to do is bake up the cookies Friday night or Saturday morning."

"Mom, I think Isabel wants everything to be homemade."

"You don't think that's going to be too much work? Making cookies and cake pops?"

"I want to show Sophie and Isabel I'm a Baking Bookworm too."

"All right. But try not to worry, okay?" She strokes my hair. "Everything will be fine. Now, why don't you go relax for a change? Read some of that book for our club, and try to forget about baked goods, okay?"

I take a deep breath. "Okay. Thanks, Mom."

❁ ❁ ❁

The next day at school, Abigail gives me the cold shoulder. I'd tried to call her Saturday night and apologize for how our practice turned out, but she didn't answer her phone.

I'm standing at her locker, trying to get her to turn around and talk to me.

"Abigail, please. I'm sorry. I really am. I know I shouldn't have let the cake take over the evening. I want to make the party coming up on Saturday really special, you know? But Friday night was for practicing, and I'm sorry I let other things get in the way."

She slams the door and turns around. "Can I ask you something, Lily?"

"Yeah. Of course."

"Do you want to be a baker or a singer?"

"You already know the answer to that question. Why are you even asking me that? Music and singing, they mean everything to me."

She gives me a look I don't like. A look that says she's disappointed in me. "Well, you're sure not acting like it."

And then she heads off to class without me.

Chapter 13

butterscotch pudding

COMFORT IN A BOWL

When school is over, I chase after Zola as she walks toward the front door. I pull her to the side of the hallway as kids rush past us.

"Hey, do you want to come over and practice tonight?" I ask. "I promise there'll be no interruptions this time. I'm really sorry about Friday night."

She sighs. "Lily, maybe this band thing isn't such a great idea. It takes work, you know? And you seem to have lots of other stuff going on."

I can't believe what I'm hearing.

"Please don't say that. I love our band." I point down at my new shoes. "See? I even bought new shoes."

When she sees my shoes, it makes her smile. Then she looks at me and says, "Dude, you gotta understand something, though. It takes more than cute shoes to make a band."

"I know," I tell her as I lightly squeeze her arm. "I'm really sorry. So will you help me talk Abigail into coming over tonight? We'll get that song finished and we will rock it. I know we will." I glance around the hallway before I say, "Don't you want to show the New Pirates they're not the only band in town?"

I can tell by the look on her face she does. "Yeah. Of course. But we all have to work at it. We each have to do our share. It's not fair otherwise."

I nod. "You're totally right. Please forgive me and let's start over, okay? We'll have an awesome practice. Just wait."

Abigail walks by just then. "Hey," Zola calls out to her. "Come here for a second."

She stops but doesn't seem too happy about it. "I need to go. My mom's waiting for me."

"Can you practice tonight?" Zola asks. "Lily feels really bad, and I think we need to give it another chance."

"I don't know," she says, fiddling with the zipper on her hoodie. "I mean, what's the point? The New Pirates are going to win. There's no way we can beat them."

I remember what my parents have been telling me all along. "So let's not worry about them. Let's just play for ourselves. I want to finish that song. I want to hear what it sounds like from start to finish, with you guys playing it. How many people can say they actually wrote a song and played it? I bet not very many, but I want to be able to do that."

Abigail looks at me and I can tell she's thinking about what I said. "Okay," she finally says. "But no phone calls or cake baking. Please?"

"Don't worry," I tell her. "No more distractions."

"What about the cupcake song?" Abigail asks, half smiling.

"I'm on it," I tell her. "Soon. I mean, probably after I get this party out of the way."

"Wait a minute," Zola says, her brown eyes big and round. "I have an idea. How about we play at the party? It'd be good practice for the audition."

Abigail's face lights up. "I love that idea. We can play 'Happy Birthday' for the birthday girl and then play our song. See what people think."

I shrug. "Okay. Yeah, we can do that. My dad will need to move the instruments upstairs for us, but I can help him. It shouldn't be a problem."

"I gotta run," Abigail says. "Later, alligators."

We wave good-bye, and as Zola and I walk outside, into the gray and cloudy March day, I'm feeling better about things than I've felt in a long time.

We head our separate ways and I feel good as I walk home.

Even when Isabel calls, I don't panic. After all, Mom and I have a plan. We know what we're doing with the food, and it's going to be amazing. I just know it. I can picture the table of sweet treats in my head. I can hear the compliments everyone gives me about the cake pops.

"Hello?" I say with a smile when I answer my phone.

"Lily, it's Isabel. I have good news! Guess what I just did!"

"What?"

"I got a band to agree to play at Sophie's birthday party. The best part is, they'll do it for free. Can you believe that?"

I stand inside the refrigerator door, letting the cold air wash over me. I feel faint. Sick. I don't want to ask the question, but I have to. Even though I'm pretty sure I know the answer.

"What's the name of the band?" I ask.

"The New Pirates. Have you heard of them? There's this kid Bryan in the band, and my dad and his dad are good friends. Bryan goes to your school. Maybe you know him? Anyway, we ran into them yesterday at the grocery store, and when his dad told us Bryan was in a band, I had the brilliant idea to ask if they might like to play at the party. He said he had to check with his bandmates. I just got off the phone with him, and they said they'd do it! They want to practice for some big audition coming up."

I grab one of the leftover bowls of instant butter-scotch pudding Mom made last night for dessert and then I shut the refrigerator door. After I get a spoon, I sink into a chair at the kitchen table.

I sigh. "Isabel, I—"

"Oh no," she interrupts. "I should have checked with you first. I'll be so sad if they can't play. I know Sophie will love having live music. I thought about asking you and your band to play, but you're hosting the party and that's enough for you to worry about. Besides, who won't love a band called the New Pirates, right? I hope it's okay. Can you check with your parents and get back to me? Please?"

My heart feels like it's a rope in a tug-of-war game. Isabel and Sophie are on one end while Abigail and Zola are pulling on the other.

Part of me wants to tell her no. The New Pirates can't play because my band should perform if we're going to have a band. The other part of me wants to tell her yes, of course the New Pirates can play, because she loves the idea, which means Sophie will love the idea, and I *really* want Sophie to be happy.

I don't know what to do. All I know is my heart

hurts from all that pulling. I can tell she is in love with this idea. Offering up my band as a replacement won't be the same. After all, her dad and Bryan's dad are friends. And Bryan's cute. I know I should say something—stand up for the Dots. But just the thought exhausts me. "Sure. I'll ask them tonight and see what they say."

"Thank you so much, Lily. You're the best. How's the food planning coming along?"

I take a bite of the pudding. It is delicious. "Mom and I are going to make cake pops. Little cake balls on sticks? Have you seen them?"

"Oh, fun! That's a great idea."

"Sophie loves chocolate-chip cookies, so we'll probably have some of those too. Don't worry. My mom and I have it under control. It's all good."

"Yay!" she squeals. "It's going to be fabulous! Oh, and I wanted to tell you, I've had seven people say they can't make it. So counting you and me, we'll have about twenty-five people there. Now all we need is a way to get Sophie to your house."

I set the spoon down and lean back in the chair. "Maybe we should talk to Sophie's mom. You know, tell her about our surprise. They might be planning a special dinner or something for her that night."

"You're probably right," Isabel says. "Should one of us call her? Or go over there? What do you think?" I start to answer, but Isabel keeps talking. "You know what? I'll just call her mom right now. I'll use my mom's cell phone. That way Sophie won't recognize the number, and if she answers, I'll just hang up."

"Good idea."

"Let's talk again tomorrow, okay? I'll tell you what her mom and I come up with and you can tell me what your parents say about the band."

"Okay. Bye, Isabel."

"Bye."

I take another bite of pudding as I think about the New Pirates playing at the party. The more I think about it, the angrier I get. Isabel should have asked me about our band. It's not right to assume I wouldn't want to do it.

Now she's pushed me into a corner, and I have to figure out how to get myself out.

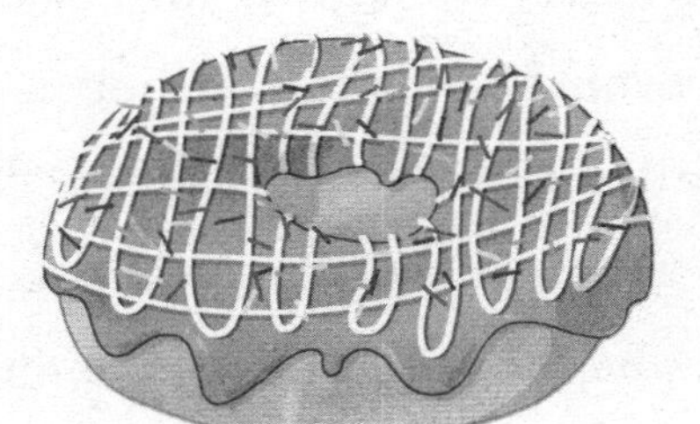

Chapter 14

strawberry-lime cupcakes

A SPECIAL AND EXCITING DESSERT

I'm in my room at my desk doing homework when my mother bursts through the door, a smile as big as the sun on her face.

"Guess what," she says.

"What?"

She doesn't answer right away. It's like she's trying to figure out if she should drag the surprise out any longer. "Who is your favorite chef on TV?"

I give her a curious look. "Chef Smiley?"

She rushes over, takes my hands, and pulls me out of my chair. She's dressed up in a suit and her long brown hair is pulled back in a bun. She must have had meetings today at work. "Yes! We're going to see him. Tonight! He's in Portland this week. The radio station is hosting a class for radio listeners, and I just won two tickets!"

My mouth drops open. "Mom, are you kidding?"

"No," she says, holding up her hand like she's being sworn into court. "I swear it's true. We need to get ready right now so we can leave in thirty minutes. It'll be rush hour soon, and we'll have to stop for dinner on the way too. So get ready and I'll see you downstairs."

She starts to leave, but I call out, "Mom. Wait! My bandmates are coming over tonight. I can't go. I promised them we'd finish our song tonight."

"Lily, this is the chance of a lifetime. Call them and explain. They'll understand. Now, please hurry. I don't want to be late."

She doesn't give me time to protest any further. Her mind is made up. We're going. And I admit, it sounds fun, but how can I let Abigail and Zola down again? I wish she'd won four tickets. I'd invite the two of them to go with us.

I get my phone and call Abigail, hoping I can figure out how to break the news to her gently. When she answers, she doesn't even say hello.

"If you're going to cancel practice tonight," she says, "I might have to take you to the zoo and feed you to the bears."

I close my eyes and wish for forgiveness. "Abigail, I'm sorry. It's just, my mom won two tickets and it's a once-in-a-lifetime chance."

"Bears, Lily. Big, hungry bears." She sighs. "Tickets? Like, concert tickets?"

I feel my chest tighten. "No."

"What kind of tickets, then?"

I open my eyes and pace the floor. "My mom won them on the radio. Isn't that cool? They were giving tickets away for a special class, and she won. She just left my room to get ready. You know, she really didn't give me a choice. I have to go."

"What kind of class?"

Obviously, she is not going to let me off the hook.

"Have you ever watched Chef Smiley on TV?"

It's silent for a few seconds. Finally, she says, "You're kidding, right?"

"He's in Portland this week, and the radio show is sponsoring a class for some of its listeners. Doesn't that sound amazing?"

I cross my fingers and hope she agrees with me.

"Wow," she says. "I guess you really do want to be a baker, don't you?"

I shake my head and plop down on my bed. She doesn't get it. "I don't want to be a baker. But I do want to be a *better* baker than I am now, which is a terrible one. What's wrong with wanting to learn how to bake?"

"Nothing, Lily, if you have all the time in the world. But you don't! Those auditions are coming up fast, and it seems like you don't even care."

"I do care. Honest."

"Then tell your mom you want to stay home and practice. Maybe she can find a friend to go with her."

I take a deep breath and try not to get upset that she's making this so difficult. "We can practice tomorrow night. You guys don't have lessons, so that should work, right? Look, I have to go. Can you call Zola and ask if we can change practice to tomorrow?"

"Lily."

"Abigail, please? If it were you, I'd understand. I'd want you to go and have a good time. It's one night. That's all. Okay?"

She pauses before she replies in a softer voice. "Okay. I'll call her. Will you be at school tomorrow?"

"Yes. We'll probably get home late, but my mom won't let me stay home. I'll see you then, okay?"

"Bye."

I hang up and rush to my closet, trying to figure out what a person should wear to meet a well-known pastry chef. I decide on a simple black jersey knit dress. I wear my new polka-dot sneakers, too, for luck. I really hope a little bit of Chef Smiley's baking skills can rub off on me.

A few hours later, we're seated in a classroom at the Western Culinary Institute. On the way over, Mom explained it's a school where people learn how to become chefs. The classroom has a counter covered with kitchen tools and ingredients. Behind the counter, along the wall, are a stove, a sink, and a refrigerator. It looks like a small kitchen in a home, but is set up so people can sit and watch what's happening in the kitchen.

I was hoping it'd be more of a hands-on class, where we'd all get to bake something, but that would probably be really hard to do.

When Chef Smiley comes out, wearing his white chef shirt, he says, "Good evening, friends. I'm so glad you're here to bake with me!" Everyone applauds.

"Tonight you're in for a real treat. Literally." He rubs his belly and laughs. "We are going to make strawberry-lime cupcakes. But as you'll see, these aren't your normal cupcakes. They have a tasty surprise in each one."

Mom and I look at each other and smile, and I admit, I'm excited. Maybe I can learn how to make fabulous cupcakes like Isabel.

Chef Smiley continues. "Before I get started, I want you to reach under your chairs. Taped to one of them is a bright orange piece of paper with a few words written on it. Everyone check, please, and if you find the piece of paper, raise it high in the air, so I can see it."

I lean to the side of my seat and then reach up and search the bottom of the chair with my hand. When I feel something on my fingertips, I have to cover my mouth with my other hand to keep from squealing.

I pull the piece of paper away from the chair and read what it says.

CHEF SMILEY'S

PERSONAL ASSISTANT

FOR THE EVENING

Mom and I look at each other again. She puts her arm around me and gives me a squeeze. "Looks like you get the best seat in the house."

"Mom, what if I mess up?" I whisper to her. "In front of all of these people? Maybe you should do it."

"It'll be fine," she says. "Don't worry. He'll help you."

I guess I don't have a choice. Everyone is looking

around, wondering who found the note. My heart races as I hold the sheet high in the air, just like Chef Smiley said to do.

"Oh, good," the chef says. "Come on up here, please. Let's meet the person who will be my helper this evening."

I force my shaky legs to stand up and somehow I make it to the front of the room without falling down. Chef Smiley directs me to go around the counter until I'm standing right next to him.

"Well, hello there," he says. He looks just as nice and friendly up close. "Can you tell us your name, good and loud, so everyone can hear you?"

"Lily."

"It's wonderful to meet you, Lily. I assume you like to bake, if you're here tonight?"

I hold on to the counter for support. "Well, I'm here because I want to be a better baker. I'm pretty much a disaster in the kitchen."

He gives me a look of concern. "Disaster? What do you mean?"

"Nothing ever seems to go right when I'm baking. I overfill the cake pans or use the wrong ingredients or I forget to do something important, like put the lid on the blender."

He puts his arm around me and talks to the audience. "I already like this girl. Don't you love her honesty?"

Everyone claps, and I feel my cheeks getting warm.

"Here's what I want you to remember, Lily. More than anything, baking should be fun. Do your best and have fun! If something doesn't turn out, well, you've learned something for the next time, right? It took a lot of years and a lot of practice for me to get to where I am now. So let's see if I can teach you a few things tonight. How do you like the sound of that?"

I nod as I feel myself relax a little bit. Chef Smiley is so nice and maybe I will learn something.

He claps his hands together. "All right, then. Let's get started. Lily, I'll have you wash your hands behind me while I go over the ingredients with our guests."

I turn toward the sink and pinch my hand to make sure I'm not dreaming. Nope. Wide awake.

This is really happening. I'm baking with a famous pastry chef. Unbelievable.

Chef Smiley talks while I turn the faucet on and pick up the bar of soap. "Lily mentioned using the wrong ingredients, and that's our first lesson tonight. It's so important to follow the recipe closely and make sure you use the correct ingredients. For example, this recipe calls for all-purpose flour, so you want to make sure that's what you're using."

I dry my hands and go back to standing next to him. He points to each ingredient, which seem to be all measured out in various-sized bowls along the counter, while he talks about each one.

"Lily," he says as he puts the beaters into the mixer, "I'm going to ask you to go through the fresh strawberries in that bowl and pick out the best ones for our recipe. While she does that, I'm going to cream the butter, sugar, and eggs until fluffy. That's another mistake people make—when mixing ingredients, don't undermix or overmix. If the recipe says this mixture should be fluffy, then I'm going to keep beating until it's fluffy. Okay?"

He passes me the bowl of strawberries before he

starts mixing the ingredients. A wave of panic washes over me. What does he mean by best? Biggest? Reddest? Juiciest?

I wait until he's done. When the mixer stops, I ask, "Um, what are you going to use the strawberries for?"

He's scraping the bowl with a spatula. "Lily, that's an excellent question. Do you know why, audience? I wasn't specific enough in my directions. If we're going to chop them up and use them in the recipe, she might choose different strawberries than if we were going to use them as a topping on the cupcake."

Chef Smiley reaches under the counter and pulls out a small plate with a pretty, frosted cupcake on it. The cupcake is cut in half, and when he spreads the halves apart, it makes me smile, because right there, in the middle of the cupcake, is a fresh strawberry, cut in half as well. When he shows the cupcake to the audience, everyone says, "Ooooh." It's pretty funny.

"After we bake the cupcakes," he explains, "we're going to cut a cone-shaped hole in each one and insert a small strawberry into that hole. We'll put our special lime buttercream frosting on the top, and you won't even know there's a strawberry inside until you bite into it." He looks at me, his green eyes sparkling. "Isn't that a fun surprise?"

"Yes, but it sounds kind of hard. How do you keep the cupcake from crumbling apart when you put the strawberry down the middle of the cupcake?"

Now he starts mixing the dry ingredients together. "It is a bit tricky. You'll want to choose strawberries that aren't too large. And you don't want to cut the hole for the berry too big. This is definitely a recipe that's easier with a friend, and one that requires you to really take your time and not rush through it."

Now that I know what kind of berries to look for, I go through the bowl and pick out the ones that are on the small side but look red and juicy.

When I'm finished, he's almost done getting the batter all mixed up. "Excellent work, Lily. Would you like to drop the batter into our cupcake pan that I've already filled with liners?"

I shake my head. "Not really. I'll just make a mess and get more batter on the countertop than in the liners."

He frowns. "Oh no. Have a bit more confidence

in yourself, my dear. We'll use a gravy ladle to scoop up the batter and then carefully pour the batter into the liners. See?" He demonstrates for us. "Easy as pie."

"Easy as pie?" I say without thinking. "Pie is totally complicated, isn't it?"

Everyone laughs.

Chef Smiley winks at me. "You're right. Baking a pie isn't exactly easy. I think the saying is referring to eating them. Now, that's easy!" He hands me the gravy ladle. "But you keep practicing in the kitchen, and I bet you'll be baking a pie in no time." He looks into my eyes and with more confidence than I've ever heard in anyone's voice, he says, "I believe in you, Lily."

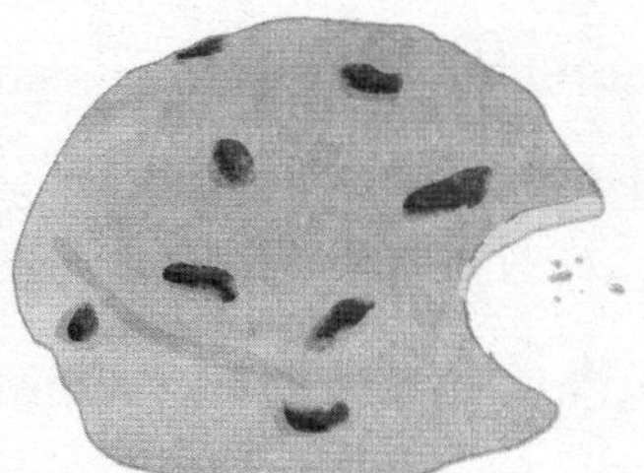

Chapter 15

fruit smoothie

EASY TO MAKE, EASY TO DRINK

At the end of the class, after Chef Smiley tastes one of the cupcakes and yells, "Sweet Uncle Pete, that's good," everyone gets a cupcake to try. Mom and I agree that the strawberry-lime cupcakes are amazing. The fresh strawberry inside each one is like nothing I've ever seen, or tasted, before.

Chef Smiley shakes hands with everyone on their way out. He asks my mom and me to step aside so he can speak to us after everyone else is gone, so that's what we do.

When he comes over to us, he says, "Lily, thank you for being a delightful assistant tonight. You did a wonderful job."

"This is my mom, Connie." Chef Smiley shakes her hand. "Thank you for everything I learned tonight. It was fun."

"I hope you'll keep practicing," he says. "I know baking can be frustrating sometimes, but it can also be very rewarding, working hard at something and then being able to share the results with people you care about."

"She tries really hard," my mom tells him as she strokes my hair. "I'm proud of how hard she tries."

"I want to give you something," he says as he steps over to the counter. He comes back carrying a book and a pen. "This is my first cookbook, coming out next month. You get one of the first copies, Lily."

He opens the cover, writes something, and then hands the book to me.

"Wow," I say. "Thank you! This will be a huge help."

He smiles. "I hope it is!"

We say good-bye and as we walk to the car, I read what he wrote. It says:

For Lily ~

It's true. One cannot live on dessert alone. But a treat now and then makes life extra sweet. Happy baking! Remember one of my favorite sayings—whatever works!

Your friend,

Chef Smiley

The next morning, Dad is up bright and early to help get me off to school, so Mom can sleep in a little bit. I wish I could have slept in too. We didn't get home until eleven, since Portland is about a two-hour drive from Willow. I feel like a stale, dried-out cupcake.

I slide into a chair at the kitchen table.

"Good morning," Dad says as he sets a glass of something purple in front of me. "I made you a smoothie. It's yogurt, a little orange juice, and frozen berries all blended together. It's kind of like a breakfast shake."

I take a sip through the straw. "Yum, Dad. And I

see you remembered to put the lid on the blender, which is always a good thing."

He chuckles before he turns back to the stove. "I'm glad you like it. I'll have your cheesy eggs ready in a minute. Did you have fun last night?"

I set the smoothie down. "Yeah. It was a lot of fun. We made cupcakes, and I got to be Chef Smiley's personal assistant."

"Cool. I bet you learned a lot, huh?"

"I guess," I say. "I'm not sure I could make those cupcakes without the chef to help me. He makes it look so easy, but it's really not easy at all."

He brings me my plate of scrambled eggs with shredded cheese melting on top of them. Curls of steam rise up from the plate. It looks delicious. I take a bite while Dad sits down across from me. "It's a lot like making music," he says. "Taylor Swift makes it look simple, but your band has probably discovered by now, it's a combination of hard work, talent, and more hard work."

"Oh, Dad, that reminds me. The Dots are going to practice tonight. Can we use your studio? We're really close to finishing a song."

He smiles. "The Dots. Nice. I like it. And yes, you can use the studio tonight for a couple of hours."

"And if we decide to play at Sophie's birthday party Saturday night, could we move the equipment upstairs? I can help you."

He raises his eyebrows at me. "You want to play at the party? You think you're ready for that?"

"After tonight, we will be. I hope. We think it's a good way for us to practice for the audition coming up soon."

"How many songs do you have ready?"

I slink down into my seat and shovel more eggs into my mouth, trying to decide how to answer that question. I finally decide I can't lie to my dad, no matter how embarrassed I am about the answer. "Um, almost one."

He looks surprised. "Almost one? As in, not even one?"

"We have a song that's almost finished. It sounds really good. Tonight we're going to finish it and then maybe we can play it on Saturday."

He leans in and looks at me with his warm brown eyes. "Lily, don't rush things, okay? Do you remember what I told you? Play because you love it, not to try and impress other people. I'd hate to see you do too much and then have regrets. I've seen far too many musicians turn away from music because they hurried things along and weren't happy with the results."

"But, Dad—"

"Honey, I know what it feels like to want to share your music with other people. To want to give and get back something in return. But I'm telling you, if you aren't ready, wait. Keep practicing. Have fun. There will be more opportunities in the future."

"You don't know that, Dad," I say as I stand up and take my dishes to the sink. "What if our band doesn't stay together? What if this is the only chance I'll ever have to be in a band?"

Dad comes over and gives me a hug. "You are so talented, Lily. You have a lifetime of singing ahead of you."

I know he's trying to be helpful, but that is so not helpful! We want to play on Saturday and I have to figure out how to make it happen. I just have to.

Chapter 16

caramel apple

ONE STICKY SITUATION

It's so hard to be a good student when you're exhausted. How do kids who are allowed to stay up late all the time do it? They must have some superpower that helps them get by on a tiny bit of sleep. I know for a fact I was not born with that superpower. I have to keep pinching myself the next day at school to stay awake. I'm happy to get to choir, because I'm pretty sure it's impossible to sing and fall asleep at the same time.

Belinda is waiting for me again before class. "So, I hear our band will be playing at your house on Saturday night."

It catches me by surprise. But then I realize Isabel had to tell Bryan where they'd be playing, and she probably asked him if he knew me.

"Maybe," I tell her. "I'm not sure yet. I still need to talk to my parents about it and see what they think."

"But they'll say yes, right? Isabel made it sound like it's practically a done deal. You must have a huge house."

"Not really. Just average, I guess. Why?"

"Isabel said she wanted us to play for at least an hour. Because once people start dancing, they'll want to keep it going for a while."

I wait for her to smile and say, "Just kidding." Except she looks totally serious. Oh my gosh. She is totally serious. Dancing? In my house? Is there enough room for that? Even if there is, that's not the kind of party I had in mind.

I feel a little sick to my stomach. "She said that?"

Belinda crosses her arms over her chest. "Why do you look so surprised? Of course people are going to want to dance when they hear us play. That's what people do at a party with a band, Lily. You didn't know that?"

I scramble to save myself from looking stupid. "No, I did. I guess I'm surprised you could perform for a full hour, that's all. Are you sure you guys can pull it off?"

The bell rings. "Don't worry about us," she says. "We know what we're doing." Before she walks away, she whispers, "Do you?"

As we take our places on the risers, I try to imagine a group of kids dancing in my living room. If we can fit everyone, how will people dance, exactly? Like at a concert, where everyone kind of bounces to the music? Or will boys and girls pair up and dance as, like, couples? And if that happens, what if they get . . . carried away? I put my hand on my stomach, because I really don't feel well.

This is the pep talk I give myself. Except it turns into more of an argument inside my head:

Calm down, Lily. Nothing is decided. You'll talk to Isabel, and you'll work everything out. Maybe you can suggest some really fun games.

Right. Because games sound so much fun compared to dancing to a live band. Lily, get real. Face the truth!

What's the truth?

If you want to give Sophie the best birthday party ever, you have to let the New Pirates play. It's what Isabel wants, and you know it'll be a party Sophie will never forget. Abigail and Zola will understand. You can get the song ready for the audition. That's the important thing anyway.

I'm relieved when Mr. Weisenheimer asks us to start singing, because it makes the noise in my brain stop. Temporarily, anyway.

After school, when I've finished eating a sliced apple with caramel dip along with some crackers, I give Isabel a call.

"Lily," she says, "please tell me your parents said the band is okay. Please? I really want to hear them play. I think Sophie will love them."

I take a deep breath. "Hi, Isabel. So, I talked to Belinda today, one of the band members of the

New Pirates. And she said you want everyone to dance. I'm not sure we have enough room for that."

She laughs nervously. "Oh, I didn't mean dance, like at the prom or something. More like at a concert. You get what I mean, right?"

"Yeah. That makes sense, I guess." I swallow hard. "Still, it seems like this party is turning into something really different from what I thought it would be. And a lot more complicated. I'm just not sure—"

She doesn't let me finish. "You know, maybe we should have the party somewhere else. I can check with some other people today and see if I can find a different place."

"But the invitations are already out," I say. "Wouldn't that be weird, to make a change now?"

"I'd have to give everyone a corrected invitation. It would mean some extra work, but I'll do it if I have to. The important thing is to give Sophie a great birthday party."

I can see it now: everyone talking about me, about how I almost ruined the surprise party for Sophie. When it's all over, what would Isabel say about me to

Sophie? Instead of growing closer to Sophie and the other girls in the book club, I'd be pushing myself farther away.

The words come rushing out, because as difficult as everything is, I think changing things now would be a lot worse. "No, it's fine," I tell her, trying not to be mad that Isabel keeps getting her way while I have to push what I want aside. "My dad said a band at the party is okay." Which is true. He just thought it would be my band.

She squeals with excitement. "Thank you so much! This party is going to be amazing. Like, the best birthday party in the history of the universe. Oh, and Sophie's mom is going to tell Sophie she's taking her out for a nice dinner, just the two of them, for some special mother-daughter time. Then she'll pretend they have to stop at your house because you have a gift you want to give the birthday girl. They'll walk into the house, we'll yell surprise, and the party begins!"

"That sounds good," I tell her. "What time should I have the New Pirates arrive?"

"I'd say seven, like everyone else. Sophie's mom

is going to get her there around seven thirty."

"Okay," I say. "So, is there anything else? If not, I'll just see you Saturday, I guess."

"Yeah, I think we're good," she says. "I'll be there around five, with the decorations."

We say good-bye, and after we hang up, I start to think about how I'm going to break the news to Zola and Abigail. I don't want to be upset with Isabel, but I can't deny that I am. She basically demanded the New Pirates play at the party. If I had said no, then I would have looked like the bad guy—or girl in this case.

I really wish she hadn't put me in this position. But here I am, and now I have to figure out what to do about it.

Do I wait for the perfect moment during practice tonight and try to break it to Abigail and Zola gently, or is it better to get it over quickly, right when they get here, kind of like ripping off a Band-Aid?

My mom is a rip-off-the-Band-Aid kind of person. I've never liked that method. I think it hurts a lot more that way.

So I decide I'll wait for the right time tonight and explain, as nicely as I can, what happened. Hopefully they'll understand. Because something tells me if they don't, the Dots may be finished before we ever had a chance to really begin.

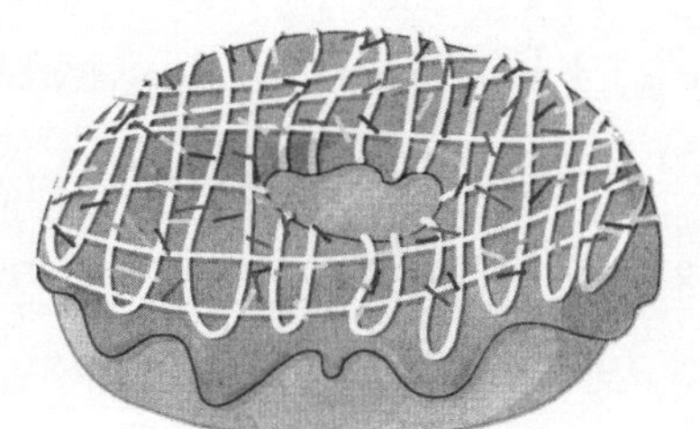

Chapter 17

hot-fudge sundaes

NO BAKING REQUIRED

After dinner, Mom brings four bowls, a half gallon of vanilla ice cream, hot fudge, and whipped cream to the table.

"Sundaes?" I ask.

"Yep," Mom says. "We have something to celebrate tonight."

I look at Dad, but he doesn't say a word. He just smiles and stands up to help scoop ice cream.

I turn to Madison. "Do you know why we're celebrating?"

She beams. "I made the varsity softball team."

"You did?" I ask. "But . . . how?"

She shrugs. "The coach said I've got what it takes."

"Madison has what you and I don't have, Lily Dilly," Dad says, drizzling hot fudge over the scoops of ice cream. "Innate athletic ability."

Mom takes a bowl from Dad and puts a dollop of whipped cream on top before she passes it to Madison. I feel anger boiling up inside of me. She wanted to play softball, she tried out for the team, and without having to practice at all, she made the team. Easy as pie.

Why is everything *so* easy for her, and why does it have to be *so* hard for me?

Mom passes me my sundae, and now I feel too upset to eat. It's not fair. Everything goes Madison's way.

Everything.

"Aren't you going to congratulate me?" Madison asks me before she takes a big bite of her sundae.

Pep talk time.

Your sister can't help it if she's naturally good at almost every-

thing. It's not her fault. It's not going to do any good to be mad at her. Remember how she was really nice to you when the chocolate cake didn't turn out? You owe it to her. Be nice. You know what Mom always says—life isn't always fair. So you have to work harder at things. Maybe that's a good thing somehow. Okay, maybe not, but still . . . do the right thing.

"Congratulations," I say as I look her right in the eyes. "I hope you make it to the championships."

"Wouldn't that be wonderful?" Mom says, sitting back down to eat her hot-fudge sundae.

I don't answer that question. But I do take a bite of my sundae, and it tastes fantastic. I think ice cream may be my new favorite dessert. After all, you don't even have to turn on the oven.

When Abigail and Zola arrive, I stay focused on finishing the song. All three of us know that's the number one priority.

It takes us a good hour to figure out the right notes and the perfect words to go with those notes, but we keep at it.

Until finally "Wishing" by the Dots is complete!

We play it three times, from start to finish, and each time, it sounds better and better.

After the third time through, Zola gives me and Abigail high fives. "Dudes, we are on our way. I can't wait for Saturday night."

Abigail grins. "Me either. Did you check with your dad? Is he cool with moving the equipment upstairs?"

"Yeah," I tell them. "But—"

I don't get a chance to finish. Zola interrupts me. "Hey, we should practice 'Happy Birthday.' We need to spice the original version up a bit. Put our own spin on it, you know?"

Abigail plays a chord on her guitar and Zola starts beating out a rhythm. It sounds so fun, I can't help but start to sing when it's time for the vocals to come in. We mess around with it for a while, and we're laughing and having such a good time, I look at my friends and think, *This is how it's supposed to be.* This is what I dreamed of when I thought about being in a band, and it's come true. It's really come true!

The moment is gone quickly, though, when Abigail looks at the clock and starts scurrying around, gathering her things. "Oh shoot. Zola, come on, we have to go. My dad is probably waiting out front for us."

The voice in my head starts screaming, *Tell them, tell them!* I need to tell them we're not playing at the party, but I can't do it. Everything has been so perfect, I don't want to ruin it.

"Bye, Lily," Abigail says as they head out the door of the studio. "Thanks for a great practice."

"See you tomorrow," Zola says.

And just like that, they're gone, and I'm left holding a song about wishing, while I'm doing a little of my own wishing.

I wish Isabel hadn't run into Bryan and his dad.

I wish the New Pirates weren't our musical enemies.

I wish we had thirty songs ready, so I could cancel the New Pirates' appearance at Sophie's party and we could easily take their place.

The more I wish, the more I realize wishing is kind of silly, because no matter how hard I wish, none of it's going to come true.

Suddenly, I'm not so sure I like the song we wrote. When you wish, you hope something good is going to happen. And when it doesn't, which is a lot of the time, then you feel bad. Like, so bad, you just want to crawl in bed and stay there.

The party is on Saturday. No matter how hard I might wish that it all goes perfectly and everyone gets along and no one is upset with me, that's probably not going to happen.

Maybe our next song should be titled "Life Isn't Fair, Deal with It."

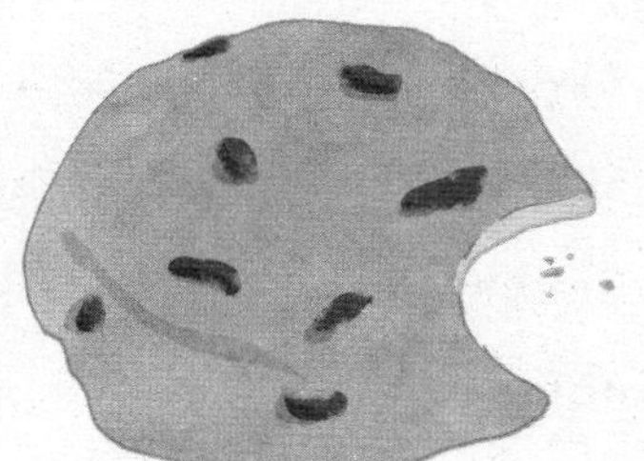

Chapter 18

candy orange slice

TASTES LIKE A SLICE OF SUNSHINE

On Tuesday, I promised myself I'd tell Abigail and Zola on Wednesday about the New Pirates playing at the party.

On Wednesday, I promised myself I'd tell Abigail and Zola on Thursday about the New Pirates playing at the party.

On Thursday, as I'm trying really, really hard to think of an excuse not to tell Abigail and Zola about the New Pirates playing at the party, I get a brilliant idea.

Both of us can play at the party! I can't believe I didn't think of it before. It makes so much sense. Isabel gets what she wants and I don't have to make any band members angry.

It's perfect!

I'm so happy and relieved, when Mom asks me if I'll go see my great-grandpa with her after school on Thursday, I don't whine or complain like I sometimes do. I just say, "Sure."

My great-grandpa Frank lives in a retirement home called New Beginnings. That means he has his own little apartment in a big building where a whole bunch of other old people also have their own apartments. The people who live there go to a big dining room three times a day for their meals. There's an activity coordinator who comes up with things for them to do. Some of the activities I've heard about are yoga, aerobics, bingo, sing-alongs, and poker night. Grandpa Frank says poker night is his favorite. He plays cards and bets with chips. The chips are like pretend money, so if he loses all of his chips, it doesn't matter. Although, he hates to lose, so I guess it does matter a little bit.

When we get to Grandpa Frank's room, Mom knocks, but the television is turned up so loud, he doesn't hear it. My great-grandma passed away a few years ago. He's lived here ever since, and I think the television may be his best friend since she died. It's kind of sad, but I guess it's good that he has something to keep him company during the day, when he's not doing some kind of activity. I told him once that he should try yoga. This is what he said: "Yoga is for young chickens. In case you haven't noticed, I am not a young chicken." I didn't argue with him, even though no one doing yoga at New Beginnings is a young chicken.

Finally Grandpa Frank opens the door and invites us in. His room smells like pine trees, like always. He buys little green trees at the store that are actually car fresheners and hangs one from the latch on one of the windows. He says the smell reminds him of the days he was a park ranger, walking around the forests of Oregon.

After he says hello and turns the television off,

he picks up the candy dish off the coffee table and offers me a candy orange slice. They are little sugary candies in the shape of an orange wedge. They're soft and chewy, sweet and delicious. And orange-flavored, of course. Every time we come to visit, I wonder if this will be the time when he doesn't have any candy in the bowl. I'd be so disappointed. But he hasn't let me down yet.

"How's the cat?" he asks.

"Good," I say. "Soft and fluffy, just the way you like him."

It makes him smile. He asks about Oscar every time we see him. He's a big fan of cats. Of all animals, really. He keeps asking the administration to make an exception and let him have his own cat, but they keep turning him down.

"You're here just in time," he tells us. He puts on a navy blue sweater-vest over his white button-down shirt and slips on his brown loafers. I guess we're going somewhere.

"In time for what?" I ask.

"They're having a sing-along downstairs."

"But you hate to sing," my mother says.

"Not since I met Betty," says Grandpa.

"Betty?" both my mom and I say at the same time.

"She sings like an angel," he says. "Just like you, Lily." He takes my hand in his and leads me to the door. "She wants to meet you."

I look at my mother, and she shrugs. What else can we do but follow Grandpa Frank to the sing-along and meet this angel named Betty?

When we get downstairs, we go to the music room. A lady is sitting at the piano flipping through sheet music, and in the center of the room are chairs in a circle. About half of them are filled with people. As soon as we walk in the room, a tall, thin woman with gray hair and a big smile outlined in red lipstick gets out of her chair and walks over to greet us.

"You must be Lily," she says to me, her hand extended. I shake it as I say, "Yes. Hi." She looks at my mom and says, "And, Connie. So nice to meet you. I'm Betty."

My mother shakes her hand and says hello.

"She's new here," Grandpa says. "Do you know what she used to do? She used to be a psychologist.

She specialized in helping people overcome their fears and achieve their dreams."

"How interesting," my mom says. "What a wonderful way to help people."

Before she can reply, Mr. Green, a longtime resident of New Beginnings, walks up to us and says, "Why did the chicken cross the road?"

"I don't know," I say like I always do when I see Mr. Green and he asks me this question. I guess it's his favorite joke, though he never gives the same answer twice.

"Well, you see, he was a rubber chicken and he wanted to stretch his legs."

It makes me smile. Mr. Green turns around and takes a seat in the circle.

"In your opinion," Mom asks Betty, "what's the biggest mistake people make when it comes to their lives and their dreams?"

"Oh, that's easy," Betty says. "They let other things get in the way. They put it off and put it off, doing other things, telling themselves it's okay because there will be time later. Really, deep down, the truth is, most of them are afraid."

"Afraid of what?" I ask.

"Oh, any number of things, I suppose. They're afraid of making mistakes. Of not getting it right the first time. Of having people make fun of them. But see, what you have to remember is that the people who made their dreams come true felt afraid too, but they didn't let it stop them. That's the difference."

The lady at the piano runs her hands across the ivory keys, and it gets everyone's attention. The four of us take a seat in the circle.

A woman wearing a purple and red dress with matching red shoes and dainty white gloves on her hands gives each of us a songbook.

"Thanks for coming today, everyone," the piano lady says. "We're going to start with 'You Are My Sunshine' on page six."

After she plays the introduction, we're all singing along. Betty is sitting beside me. When I glance over at her, I notice how her pretty green eyes sparkle like emeralds and she sings with a slight grin. Her voice is smooth and nice, but it's the happiness I notice the most. Anyone could look at her and tell that she loves to sing.

And when I look at Grandpa Frank, he is a picture of happiness too. He doesn't care if he can't sing a single note on key. He's here and there's music and Betty's smiling. There's a lot for him to be happy about.

I close my eyes for a moment, and as I start to sing, I know that for now, I don't have to try to chase away a bunch of worries about a hundred different things. It's just me and the cheerful, sweet song. Every cell in my body remembers how much I love this—music and singing.

And I never want to forget how it feels.

Chapter 19

chocolate-chip brownies

CHOCOLATE CURES ALMOST EVERYTHING

An hour of singing with a bunch of people who are not young chickens but are nice to be around anyway seems to be just what I needed. On Friday, I float through the day, hardly a care in the world. I tell Belinda to be at my house at seven o'clock Saturday night, with all of their equipment.

She says, "I'm so glad you changed your mind." Like I had a choice?

Friday evening, right after dinner, Madison takes me grocery shopping because Mom is busy closing a deal. Whatever that means. I think it means she's sold a house. Or almost sold a house and is trying to get the paperwork signed to make it official.

Madison is a huge help and suggests items I hadn't even thought of getting, like some cartons of lemonade so we have something to drink besides water. We also buy paper plates, cups, and napkins, and all of the stuff I need to make the cake pops and cookies.

"Are you feeling pretty good?" Madison asks on the drive home. "About the party?"

"I think so."

"Mom's going to help you make the cake pops?"

"Yes. We're going to do that tomorrow. Tonight I'm baking the chocolate-chip cookies."

Madison turns on her blinker before turning onto our street. "I saw Mom had a cleaning lady come today. That was a smart thing to do. I was worried we'd be up until midnight tonight, dusting and vacuuming."

"Wow, talk about a fun Friday night," I tease.

"Are you guys gonna play games at the party or what?" she asks.

"I don't know. Isabel had that on her to-do list, but we never talked about it. Do you know any good ones?"

She pulls into the driveway. "Let's see. How about pass the orange? You use either your feet or your neck to pass the orange from person to person. No hands allowed."

"That sounds hard," I say, trying to imagine playing that game with Sophie's friends. "And awkward."

A sudden wave of panic washes over me. I'm not going to know most of the kids at the party. They'll all be from Sophie's school. I'll know Sophie and Isabel, of course. And the other two girls from the book club, Katie and Dharsanaa, will probably be there. But that's it. I'm going to have a bunch of strangers in my house. Everyone will know everyone, except me. That seems so . . . weird. At least Abigail and Zola will be there. It makes me more thankful than ever that I kept quiet about the whole band thing.

Madison turns the car off. "You guys could go on a scavenger hunt. You know, come up with lists of random items like dice and rubber bands and a stuffed rabbit or whatever. Then break up into groups and go around the neighborhood to find the stuff. First group back wins."

"I don't know," I say. "We might not have that much time. I mean, the New Pirates are going to be playing for an hour."

She gives me a funny look. "The New Pirates? Who are they?"

"A band."

"And Mom and Dad said that's okay?"

"Well, Dad said my band could play, but then Isabel wanted this other band, so I'm sure it's fine."

Now Madison looks really confused. "Why isn't your band playing?"

I open the car door. "We're going to play too." I sigh. "It's a long story. And it's not really important now. Come on. Help me carry this stuff inside."

When we get to the kitchen, something smells really good. Dad is there, pulling a pan out of the oven.

"What is that?" Madison asks.

"Your mother is really stressed out," he says. "I found a box of chocolate-chip brownie mix in the cupboard, so I decided to whip up a batch." He smiles. "You know, because chocolate makes everything better. Or so I've heard, anyway."

"Wow, Dad," I say as I peer in the pan. "They look really good. Maybe you should help me with the cake pops tomorrow instead of Mom."

"Sorry, kiddo. I won't be here. Another band had to back out of a wedding reception due to illness, so we're filling in. It's a couple of hours away, which means I'm going to have to leave here in the morning, and I won't be back until tomorrow night." He rubs my head as he walks by. "I'm sure you and your mom are going to do a fantastic job. Those brownies need to cool for thirty minutes, so don't have any yet, okay?"

Both Madison and I nod. "Man, they smell amazing," she says after he's gone.

"I know," I say, my stomach begging for one. "I'm so impressed Dad made them."

"Well, I'm going to go change and then I'm out

of here," Madison says. "I'm meeting up with some friends at the movies."

"Okay," I say. "Hey, are you going to be around here tomorrow? In case Mom and I need some help?"

She shakes her head. "No way. I told you, I'm staying far, far away from here. You and Mom are on your own."

"Madison, come on," I say, giving her a little shove. "That's mean."

She laughs. "Well, even if I wanted to help, I can't. I have a preseason doubleheader tomorrow afternoon that the coach set up. She wants to move us around to different positions and figure out where we play best.

"It'll be okay," she says as she reaches for the silverware drawer and pulls out a knife. "I'm sure everything will be fine."

She goes to the pan and cuts into the brownies. "Hey, it hasn't been thirty minutes yet," I say.

She takes a bite of the ooey, gooey brownie that's falling apart in her hands. She catches a big chunk that falls off as it drops toward the floor and pops it in her mouth.

"Mmmm. Good," she mumbles. "See? It's gonna be a piece of cake. Nothing to worry about, Lily Dilly."

I nod as she heads out of the kitchen, leaving me alone with the big pan of brownies. I'm going to be good and wait the right amount of time before I have one, like Dad said.

If there's one thing I've learned, it's that things turn out best when you follow the instructions. Now, if only I had instructions for how to make a surprise party turn out perfectly from start to finish, I'd be set.

I guess I'll just have to cross my fingers and hope for the best.

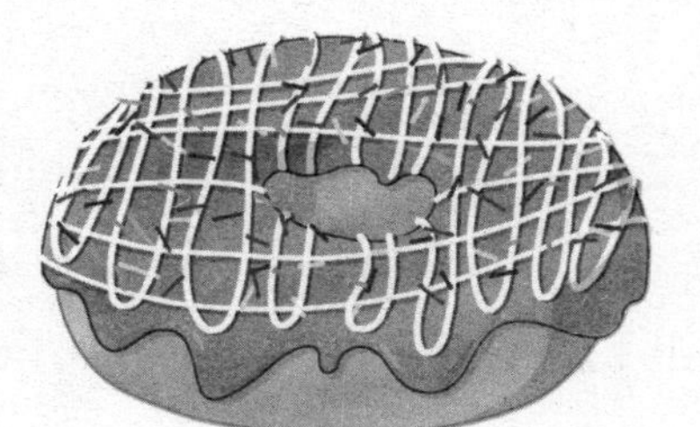

Chapter 20

chocolate-chip cookies

SWEET PERFECTION

When I wake up Saturday morning and see my alarm clock says 10:15, I jump out of bed. I didn't mean to sleep so late. It must have been because I had trouble falling asleep the night before, thinking about the party.

I make my way downstairs, but no one is around. It seems strange. I go back upstairs and find the door to my parents' bedroom shut. I knock softly. "Mom? Are you in there?"

I hear a soft moan and then, "Yes. Lily, come in."

I open the door and see her curled up, under the covers. This is not like my mother. She's always the first one up on Saturdays, with a to-do list a mile long and lots of energy to get it all done.

"Mom, are you okay?"

She doesn't move. "Don't come any closer, sweetie. I have the stomach flu, and I don't want you to get sick."

I can feel my heart racing. This is not good. In fact, it's terrible. "Are you sure? I mean, maybe you just ate too many brownies."

She chuckles. "I wish, but I don't think so. I have a fever. And I'm achy."

"Where's Dad?"

"He left a little while ago. He told you about the wedding reception, right? I'm sorry, Lil. You're going to have to make the cake pops by yourself."

"Mom, I don't think—"

"You can do it. I saw the cookies you made last night, and they turned out great. Did you try one?"

"Yeah. They're really good."

"See?" she says. "You're halfway there. Now close the door and go downstairs. If I rest, maybe I'll feel better and can help you this afternoon."

If she has a fever, that seems like wishful thinking. But I don't say anything. I don't want to make her feel any worse than she already does.

"Can I get you anything?" I ask, feeling slightly sick myself that this is happening on the worst possible day.

"No, I'm fine. Don't worry about me. I know you have enough on your plate today."

After I close the door, I try to give myself a pep talk, but I'm freaking out so much, it's impossible. No amount of pep talking is going to keep me calm right now.

I run into my room, shut the door, and yell into my pillow. It helps. A little. When I sit up, I ask myself what it is that I need more than anything. And an answer pops into my brain right away.

I need a friend. Someone who will help me get the cake pops ready, but more than that, someone who will help me get through the day without falling apart like a really dry cupcake. I need someone to help me keep it together.

I go to the phone and call Abigail.

"Hello?"

"Oh good, you're home."

"Hey. What's going on? You excited about tonight?"

"I have a huge favor to ask you," I say as I sit on my bed. "Can you come over and help me bake some cake pops?"

She laughs. "You just will not let this baking thing go, will you?"

"My mom was going to help me," I explain, "but she's sick. And I already promised Isabel we'd have cake pops at the party. She was really excited about them when I told her. Please, Abigail? It'd mean a lot to have you here."

"Okay," she says. "I'll have one of my parents bring me over after lunch. Is that enough time?"

"I think so. We need to have everything done by five, when Isabel is scheduled to get here with the decorations."

"Oh yeah, we can do it," she says. "Piece of cake."

I'm starting to get a little bit annoyed by that saying.

"Thanks, Abigail. See you in a while."

"Okay, bye."

I quickly take a shower and get myself ready. I throw on old clothes, since I'll be baking all afternoon. I can change later, after Isabel and I finish decorating the house.

When I go back downstairs, I find Madison, dressed in her softball uniform, rummaging around in the refrigerator.

"Mom's sick," I tell her.

She turns around, holding a small bottle of orange juice, and shuts the fridge door.

"Yeah. I know. I'm sorry, Lil. You gonna be okay? I hope you have a backup plan in case your cake pops don't turn out."

I cross my arms over my chest. "Backup plan? You think I'm going to need a backup plan? Thanks a lot, Madison."

"Hey," she says as she twists the lid off of the bottle, "it's good to be prepared. That's all I'm saying."

"Well, I don't have a backup plan, so be quiet. Abigail's coming over in a little while to help me make the cake pops. Together, we'll be fine."

She takes a long drink of her juice before she asks, "Where's the band going to set up? They're bringing their own equipment, right?"

"Yeah. I've been thinking about where to put them, and I think maybe the garage is the best place. I mean, you know how Dad is. It's spotless out there, and it's bigger than any room in the house. We can put some balloons and streamers out there too, right?"

She shrugs. "Whatever you want to do. It's your party." She starts to leave and then she turns around and says, "So did the other band say they were fine with your band using their instruments? Because some people are really uptight about that kind of thing, you know."

I gulp. "No. I just assumed they would let us use their equipment. I thought it would be easier that way."

"You didn't ask them?" I shake my head. "Are they good friends of yours?"

I'm pretty sure my sister can tell by the look on my face the answer to that question is a big, fat no.

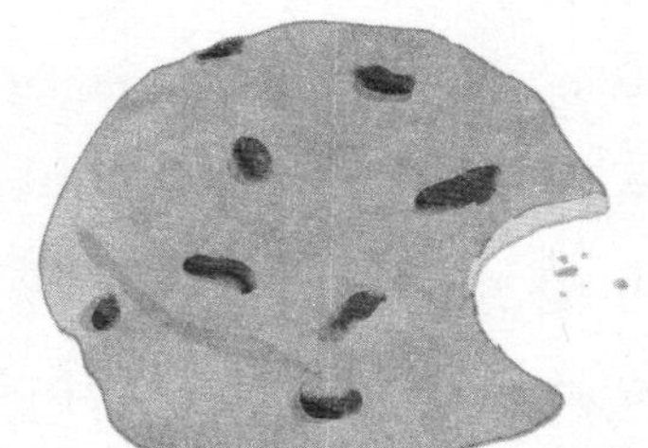

Chapter 21

lollipops

HAPPINESS ON A STICK

I remember that I'd talked to Dad about moving his studio equipment upstairs for the party before I found out the New Pirates were going to play. My heart skips a beat at the thought that maybe he remembered to move the equipment before he left this morning. It's not anywhere in the house, so I cross my fingers as I check the garage. But it's empty. He forgot. And I didn't think to ask him.

Just as I'm shutting the door to the garage, my phone vibrates in my pocket.

"Hi, Dad," I say. "I was just thinking about you."

"Lily, I'm so sorry. I forgot to ask you if your band had decided to play tonight. Was I supposed to move the equipment and instruments upstairs for you?"

I sink down into the sofa in the family room and lean my head back. Then I tell him about the New Pirates and the plan to have them play and how I was hoping our band could play too.

"What do you think?" I ask. "Will they let us use their stuff?"

"I doubt it. Most people are really protective of their instruments. It's kind of like letting some-one else drive your really fancy sports car when you don't know if her driving skills are any good."

"But we won't break anything," I say, trying to keep the tears back.

"You can't promise that, sweetie," he says softly. "I know you'd be really careful, but what if some-thing did happen? It'd be pretty horrible, right?"

"Zola and Abigail really wanted to play tonight. I don't know how I can tell them the whole deal is off.

Abigail's going to be here soon to help me, since Mom is sick."

"You're just going to have to tell them. And please apologize for me. It's partly my fault."

"Okay," I mutter.

"And, Lily, I know I probably don't have to tell you this, but you kids can't move that equipment. It needs to stay in the studio. Understand?"

"Yes."

"Look, I have to go. We stopped to get gas, and the guys are ready to roll. I'm really sorry. But don't let this ruin the party, okay? You'll have other opportunities to perform."

"Bye, Dad."

"Bye."

I make myself eat some cheese and crackers and a banana because I know hunger doesn't help my mood. When I'm finished, I check on my mom. She's sleeping, so I tiptoe out of the room and quietly shut the door.

Abigail arrives a little while later. She knows right away that something is wrong.

"Uh-oh. Are you feeling sick too?" Abigail asks.

"Not that kind of sick."

She grabs my hands. "Come on. It's not that bad. We are going to make the best cake pops you've ever seen. It'll be okay. I know you're probably worried they're not going to turn out, but you really shouldn't be. I've come prepared."

She reaches into the bag she's carrying and pulls out a pink and white apron, a bag of lollipops, and something else. It's white and shaped like an egg.

"What is that?" I ask.

"My mom's lucky timer."

"Why's it lucky?"

"Because nothing has ever burned when she's used this timer. It's like . . . magic."

"What are the lollipops for?"

"My backup plan. If the cake pops are a disaster, you just serve lollipops instead. They're cute and delicious too, right?"

It makes me smile. She is trying so hard to help me and to cheer me up. She loops her arm through mine and says, "Come on. Let's get baking!"

Abigail is being really sweet and I'm already feeling better. I know it's time to tell her the news and get it over with. Then we can focus on the cake pops.

"I need to tell you something," I say when we reach the kitchen. "I have some bad news."

She sets her bag on the kitchen table and then walks over and places the timer on the counter. "What?"

"My dad left this morning to play at a wedding reception this afternoon, and he forgot to move the instruments and equipment upstairs."

"What do you mean?"

"I mean we can't play. We can't play our songs at the party tonight."

Abigail's face droops like a wilted daisy. "We can't move the stuff ourselves?"

I shake my head. "He specifically told me not to. I'm really sorry, Abigail. He feels bad, and so do I."

She takes a deep breath. "Oh well. Guess there's nothing we can do then."

There's one more thing I have to do. A part of me is still hoping I can convince Belinda and the rest of the band to let us use their instruments when they're done. It's going to be tricky, trying to get my friends to come to the party when they don't even know Sophie. But I want to try. I don't know what they'll say when they find out the New Pirates are playing and we aren't, but I figure I'll deal with that later. One thing at a time, like my mom always says.

"I still want you and Zola to be here tonight," I tell Abigail. "I don't know most of the kids coming and I'd love it if you'd stay and hang out. Keep me company."

She slips the apron over her head and ties the straps behind her back. "You don't think your friend would mind, when she doesn't even know us?"

"Oh no. She's really nice. I can tell her you're my helpers. Or something."

She shrugs. "I don't have anything better to do. My dad is going to pick me up at four. I'll go home, eat dinner, and come back. You should call Zola and tell her we're not playing. She might be upset if she shows up here and finds out."

"Okay. I'll give her a call while the cake is in the oven."

Abigail claps her hands together. "All right. Get your apron, Lily. You think Chef Smiley's a genius in the kitchen? Well, he'll be shaking in his boots when the entire state of Oregon is talking about our magnificent cake pops."

I giggle. "Shaking in his boots? He's a pastry chef, not a cowboy, silly."

"Fine. He'll be shaking in his chef's hat. Or apron. Whatever. He's gonna be scared—that's what I'm trying to say."

Abigail's confidence makes me feel like I can do anything. Like I'm putting on a cape instead of an apron. Now let's just hope her superfriend powers combined with the magical egg timer work!

Chapter 22

cake pops

ALL THE RAGE, LITERALLY

While the cake bakes in the oven, I call Zola and tell her the bad news. She's disappointed we won't be playing, but I beg her to come anyway, and she finally gives in.

I also get my mom's laptop and look up the video on how to make cake pops and show it to Abigail. We watch it three times.

"Piece of cake," she says once again, like it's the funniest thing ever.

That joke is really getting old.

I also show her the cookbook Chef Smiley gave me.

"Whatever works?" she asks when she reads the page that he signed. "What does that mean?"

"If there's an easier way to do something, even if it's not fancy or the most popular way, it's okay. You shouldn't feel bad about doing something that works for you."

The egg timer lets out a really loud, annoying screech, making us both jump.

She runs over and turns it off while I check the oven. "So that's why it's magic," I say. "That thing's loud enough to let the people across the street know the cake's done."

"Exactly," she says.

The chocolate cake looks good. It's a little lop-sided, but it doesn't bother me at all because I know it doesn't matter.

While the cake cools, I find a tablecloth and throw it on the dining room table. Abigail helps me arrange the plates, napkins, cups, and silverware.

Then we go to work making the cake balls, following the instructions in the video. When we have four dozen and the bowl is empty, I stick them in the freezer to harden for an hour.

"Man, baking is exhausting," Abigail says as she plops down at the kitchen table. She reaches back and tightens up her ponytail.

"Thanks for helping me," I say as I sit down across from her. "It means a lot."

"We're halfway there, right?" she says. "We'll get the chocolate candies melted, do some dipping, and we're done. You can finally call yourself a baker, Lily! Just like you've wanted, right?"

I smile. "Yeah. I guess I can."

The doorbell rings.

"Who's that?" Abigail asks me as I stand up.

"I have no idea."

Abigail comes with me. When I peek out the peephole, I see Bryan standing there, his hands in his jeans pockets, looking as cute as ever.

"Hey," Bryan says after I open the door. "I know I'm way early, but my dad said it'd be a good idea to come and get everything set up now. I hope it's okay.

I figured you'd be here, getting ready for the party."

Abigail looks at me. And then back at Bryan. "What's he talking about?"

"I'll tell you in a minute," I say quickly before I step outside. It's nice today. Sunny and warm, a rare thing in March in Oregon. "Let me punch in the code and open the garage door for you." I shut the front door and hustle over to the garage. Fortunately, Mom's car is parked in the driveway, and since both Dad and Madison are gone, the garage will be empty.

"You sure the garage is the best place for us?" Bryan asks as I punch in the code that opens the door.

"I'm sure," I say, hoping he approves of the space.

After the door is up, he stares at the neatly organized shelves along the walls. "Ah. I see. Your dad's a neat freak. It's perfect."

He motions to his dad, who's in a white van parked in front of our house, to pull into the driveway.

"Well, let me know if you need anything," I tell him. "I'll be inside, making cake pops."

He gives me a curious look. "Cake pops? What's that, cake mixed with soda pop or something?"

Oh brother. "Never mind. Just shut the door when you're done, okay?"

I head back toward the house, when he calls out, "Hey, Lily?"

I turn around and face Bryan. "Yeah?"

"I think it's really great you're letting us play when you're probably bummed and wishing your band could play. What's your band's name again?"

"The Dots."

"Nice. Anyway, I want you to know, we'll make it a fun party. I promise."

It's a kind thing to say, and I'm glad he's not rubbing it in my face. But right now, with Abigail inside probably fuming about this whole thing, I wish more than anything that we were playing instead. I wave to Bryan and run back inside the house.

"Lily," Abigail says with her arms crossed over her chest, "please tell me the New Pirates are not playing at this party tonight."

"I wish I could," I say softly, "but they are playing."

She starts to say something else, but I keep going. "Isabel's dad knows Bryan's dad. She asked Bryan about playing at the party before she said anything to me. She was so excited about them playing, I couldn't say no. I mean, you should have heard her, Abigail. She wouldn't stop talking about the New Pirates and how good-looking Bryan is and how much Sophie will love having them play for her thirteenth birthday."

"So how long have you known about this?"

"For a while," I say. "The thing is, I thought we could play too. That way everyone would be happy. Until I found out that bands don't really like other bands to use their instruments."

Abigail walks past me without another word and into the kitchen. I follow her like a puppy with its tail between its legs. She takes her apron off and stuffs it into her bag, and then she gets the magical egg timer and the lollipops and puts those in the bag too.

"Where are you going?" I ask.

"Home."

"Abigail, wait, please."

She turns and looks at me. "You should have told us about the New Pirates."

"You're right. I'm sorry."

"I feel like I don't know you anymore, Lily. What's happened? Ever since you decided to have this party, it's like you're a different person. I hope you have fun tonight, with your other friends, since them and baking seem to be more important than anything to you."

And then she's gone. I think about chasing after her, but I can tell it wouldn't do any good. She's too mad right now.

I blink back tears as I slink into the living room and collapse on the couch, thinking about what Abigail said. Have I become a different person? Did I go too far with this party, wanting so badly for it to be the very best it could be for Sophie?

Maybe I did, but that's because I care about her. I care about Abigail and Zola too, though. Don't they know that?

An image of Abigail's face, covered in sadness, pops into my head. Obviously, she didn't know, because I did a terrible job of showing them.

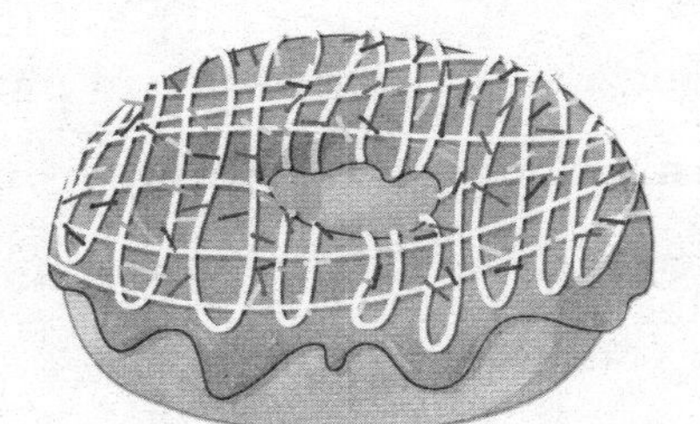

Chapter 23

chocolate

DELICIOUS HOT OR COLD

After I let myself pout for a little while, I go upstairs to check on Mom. She's fast asleep, and as much as I want to wake her and tell her what's happened, I know she needs her rest.

I'm on my own.

As I'm heading back to the kitchen to finish making the cake pops, there's a knock at the door.

Hoping it's Abigail, I rush to the door and fling

it open. But it's not Abigail. It's Bryan.

"Oh. Hi," I say.

He gives me a concerned look. "Hi. Are you okay?"

I try to smile. "Yeah. Fine. Are you all set up?"

"Almost. I forgot an extension cord and wondered if you might have one we could borrow."

I could be mean and say no and slam the door in his face, after everything that's happened. But I'm not going to do that. It's not his fault that I've messed up so badly with my bandmates. "Sure. Come in. I think my dad has some extras in his studio."

He steps into the entryway and I point him to the kitchen and tell him he can get a glass of water if he's thirsty, while I go down to the studio.

"I smell chocolate," he says when I come back. I watch as he surveys the kitchen, which is a mess right now. "Is it those cake pops you were talking about?"

I hand him the cord. "Yeah. They're in the freezer right now. I need to finish them. Abigail was supposed to help me but . . . she left."

He leans up against the counter. "I saw her leave. She didn't look very happy. Was she mad about something?"

"You could say that."

"Let me guess," he says, sweeping the bangs out of his eyes. "She's mad you guys aren't playing tonight?"

I look down at my shoes and nod. It's so embarrassing, talking to him about this.

"I'm sorry," he says. And the way he says it, I know he means it. "Is there anything I can do? Want me to stay and help you?"

I jerk my head up, surprised by his offer. "Really? You'd do that?"

He shrugs. "Sure. Let me finish in the garage and then I'll tell my dad I'll walk home when we're done."

After he leaves, I go to work cleaning off the counters and making room for the next part of the process: icing and decorating the pops. The whole time I'm thinking how nice Bryan is to offer to stay and help me. I'm kind of nervous about him seeing me fumble around in the kitchen, but I know the extra set of hands will be worth it.

I get out the double boiler, fill the bottom of the pan with water, and put it on the stove. While I wait for the water to boil, I take the cake pops out of the freezer and put the sticks in them. When Bryan knocks on the door again, I run to let him in and then lead him to the kitchen and show him what we'll be doing.

After the water boils, I put the white-chocolate candy pieces in the pan that sits on top of the pan of hot water. The heat from the hot water below is what will melt the chocolate.

"Can you stir while I add in the food coloring?" I ask.

He takes the wooden spoon from me and I pick up the little bottle with a red cap. I squirt in a few drops while he stirs. It becomes a pretty pink color.

"So now what?" he asks.

"Now we roll each ball of cake in the melted chocolate and then in some sprinkles. Oh, wait, I need to put the decorations in bowls."

"Where do we set the cake pops to dry?" he asks, still stirring. "If we lay them down on the counter, one side will be smooshed, you know? I'm guessing smooshed isn't the look you're going for."

He's right. I remember the lady in the video stuck the cake pops in a piece of Styrofoam so they could stand straight up as they dried. I'm looking around the kitchen as I'm pouring sprinkles into bowls, trying to think of something that would work as well as a piece of Styrofoam. But I can't think of anything.

"This chocolate is getting pretty hot," he says. "Should I turn off the heat?"

"Um, I don't think so," I say, opening a cupboard door full of bowls. "We don't want the chocolate to harden. Maybe turn it down a little bit?"

I'm staring into the cupboard when he says, "What about that thing?"

"What thing?" I ask.

He points at the top shelf. "I don't know what it's called. You put spaghetti noodles in it so the water drains? Here, let me get it."

He reaches up and takes out the silver colander. By turning it upside down, he's created a dome of holes and I realize it's perfect. "You are a genius, Bryan."

A smile spreads across his face. "Well, thanks. Pretty sure that's the first time I've heard my name and the word 'genius' in the same sentence."

"Come on," I say. "Help me roll the balls in the chocolate."

"I'll watch you do it first," he says. "To make sure I do it right."

"I've never made them before, so I'm not really

an expert," I tell him as I pick up a cake pop. "Cross your fingers it works!"

I roll the ball through the melted chocolate and then roll it around in some green sprinkles. When I turn the cake pop upright so I can put it in the colander to cool, the whole ball slides down the stick.

"Oh no," I say. "What'd I do wrong?"

"Maybe you need to work faster," he says. He does one and goes through the motions much faster, but this time the cake ball falls apart before he even rolls it in the sprinkles.

I can't believe this is happening. My chest tightens and it takes every ounce of strength I have not to burst into tears in front of him.

"I think the chocolate may be too hot," he says as he turns the burner off. "Let's keep trying."

Again and again, the cake balls either fall apart or slide down the stick. I wash my hands before I sink into the kitchen chair, checking the clock on the microwave. It's just after four o'clock. We have less than an hour to pull some amazing dessert out of thin air.

Bryan pops one of the cake balls into his mouth. "They taste pretty good," he says. I can tell he's trying to make me feel better, but it's not working.

"I'm such an idiot," I say, putting my face into my hands. "Why did I think I could pull this off?"

Bryan comes over and sits across from me. "Lily? Are you okay?"

I shake my head.

"Do you have any other food?"

I look up at him. "I made chocolate-chip cookies last night. But this is a birthday party. A surprise birthday party! I should have an amazing dessert for Sophie, and I have . . . nothing."

With a crooked smile he says, "At least you have an amazing band, right?"

Before I can tell him it's so funny I forgot to laugh, the doorbell rings. I get up and Bryan follows me.

When I open the door, the situation goes from bad to worse.

Isabel, Katie, and Dharsanaa are on my porch. The silver balloons they brought float above them.

"Hi, Lily," Isabel says, holding a giant shopping bag in one hand and a big bowl of caramel corn in the other. "Are you ready to make Sophie over-the-moon happy with the best surprise party ever?"

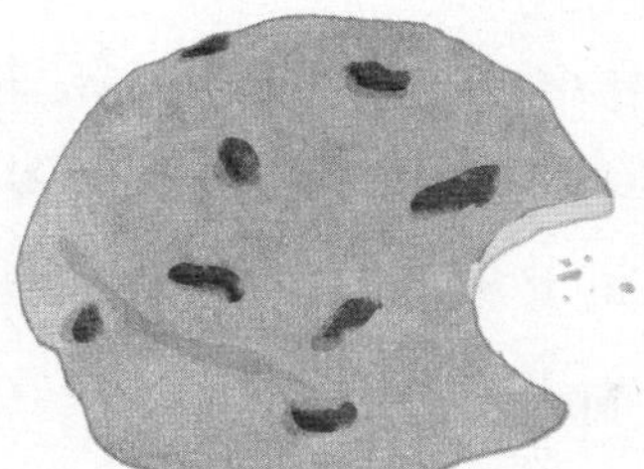

Chapter 24

caramel corn

A PERFECT ADDITION TO ANY PARTY

I stand there with my mouth open, unable to speak.

"I know we're early," Isabel says, "but I wanted to make sure we had plenty of time to get things ready. Oh, and I hope it's okay that I brought a couple of helpers along. And some homemade caramel corn."

I think I might be sick. And not because of the

caramel corn, which I love. Somehow I manage to say, "Yeah, it's fine."

We stand there a few seconds, looking at each other, and it feels like my heart is going to pop right out of my chest, it's beating so hard. All I can think is, *What am I going to do? What am I going to do?*

"So, can we come in?" Katie asks with a nervous giggle.

"Oh, sorry. Yes, please."

Once they're inside, I take the bowl from Isabel and introduce them to Bryan. I explain that he came over early to set up the band equipment and then stayed to help me with the cake pops.

"Can we see them?" Isabel asks. She looks at Bryan as she says, "I bet they're perfect!"

He doesn't say anything, just raises his eyebrows and looks at me to answer.

My brain is scrambling, trying to figure out how I can get out of this awful situation. But there's no way out. The Baking Bookworms are here and the kitchen looks like a tornado has hit, and I know I have to tell them the truth.

"Follow me," I say.

When we get into the kitchen, I set the bowl down on the counter and watch the three girls as they take in the sight of abandoned cake balls and empty sticks all over the countertops.

Isabel's mouth drops to the floor. "What happened?"

"Something went wrong," I tell them. "I'm not sure what I did. All I know is the cake pops didn't turn out. I should have practiced making them first. I'm so sorry, you guys. I wasn't honest with you. I'm a terrible baker. I try and I try, and every time, something like this happens."

They look horrified. It's like I've told them there are zombies trying to break down the front door. "So, we have no food?" Isabel asks.

"There's still time," Bryan says. "We can run to the bakery." He looks at me. "Can't we? Is your mom or dad here?"

"My dad's out of town and my mom's upstairs, sick with the flu."

Now Isabel is the one who looks sick. "Lily, you have to do something. I've worked so hard to get people here, get a band, and all you had to do was make a dessert. Sophie's party is ruined unless you think of something fast."

The way she says it, like I had the easy part, makes me upset. "You asked me to cohost this party. To have it here, at my house. You've barely let me have a say in *anything*. I would have bought a nice cake and some other treats at the bakery, but you didn't think that was special enough. And then there's the band. Did you ever think about what it would be like for me to have to listen to another band play at my house? My friends are mad at me because you just had to have the New Pirates play at this party." I take a deep breath. "I've worked so hard to make this party the best it could be. And you're saying it's going to be a failure because one thing didn't go right? Well, it's not going to be a failure. Sophie is going to have a great birthday party. Just wait and see."

It's quiet for a few awkward seconds before Bryan claps his hands together and says, "Okay, you know what I want to do? I want to hang some streamers. It's, like, my favorite thing in the world. Come on, Isabel. You must have brought some streamers, right? Let's go. Everything's going to be fine. Streamers will help. You'll see."

I turn around and go to work cleaning the kitchen. Bryan's chatting up a storm with the other girls, trying to lighten the mood, as they go through the decorations Isabel brought along. We become robots, doing what we need to do to get the place ready. As I clean, I try to think if there's anything I can make quickly with the ingredients on hand. I check the flour and sugar containers and remember I used the last of our supply when I baked the cookies last night. And we don't have any cake mixes in the pantry, so whipping up a cake isn't a possibility.

As I pull out the containers of chocolate-chip cookies, I spy the pan of brownies Dad made last night. I have four dozen cookies and probably a dozen brownies. There's got to be something I can do with them to turn them into some kind of fun dessert. I think and I think, and then an idea comes to me. The question is, can I make it work?

I run upstairs to Mom's office and get a huge cardboard box she folded up and put in the closet. Before I go downstairs, I peek in and check on her. She's awake and so I take a minute to tell her what happened, along with my latest and greatest idea.

"I'm proud of you, Lily," she says. "I think it sounds fabulous."

I run downstairs and cut one of the sides off of the box. Then I cover the large piece of cardboard with aluminum foil and set it in the middle of the dining room table. I line up the brownies from top to bottom to make a gigantic number one. Next to it, I put the cookies in the shape of a number three.

"Wow," Isabel says behind me. "A sweet thirteen. It looks amazing, Lily."

"Yeah. I made the chocolate-chip cookies last night, since they're Sophie's favorite dessert. It's kind of a fun creation, right?"

She softly says, "They're Sophie's favorite? Really? I don't think I knew that."

I shrug. "One of them, yeah." I continue. "We have lots of vanilla ice cream and hot fudge sauce. After Sophie blows out her candles, everyone can make a brownie or cookie sundae. Does that sound okay?"

She nods, and I see tears forming in her eyes. "I'm

really sorry. About everything. I wanted to show Sophie how much she means to me, you know?" She looks down and picks at her thumbnail. "I was afraid I was losing her to you. That's why I got the New Pirates to play and not your band."

I stand there, my mouth gaping open. I can't believe she was worried about losing her best friend to me. I'm the one who's the outsider. The one who wants so badly to fit in with the Baking Bookworms.

"And I'm sorry I didn't say anything about my horrible baking skills," I say. "I didn't want you guys to kick me out of the book club. I really want to be a part of it."

"So, can we start over?" Isabel asks. "Put the stupid jealousy behind us and just be friends?"

I point to the number thirteen made out of brownies and cookies. "That's one thing I'm really good at," I say, smiling. "Starting over."

Chapter 25

brownie sundaes

A GREAT WAY TO SAY "SURPRISE!"

Purple streamers twist and turn through the air, to the center of the dining room, where they gather at the sparkly chandelier. A dozen silver balloons, filled with helium, bob across the ceiling, with long, curly ribbons in a variety of colors streaming down from each one. We also hung strips of streamers in the doorways and other spaces throughout the bottom floor of the house, like curtains. It looks really cool.

The garage is decorated with streamers and balloons as well. And we moved an area rug from the basement to the garage, to make it feel more comfortable—less like a garage and more like a bonus room.

Mom came downstairs in her pink bathrobe to refill her water cup just as I was getting ready to go and change out of my grubby clothes and into my purple and black striped dress. The look on her face as she scanned the decorations and treats told me we had done a fantastic job.

Now Isabel and I are greeting kids as they arrive, taking their gifts and putting them on the coffee table in the family room. I totally forgot to get Sophie a gift. When I ran upstairs to ask Mom, who'd gone back to bed, if we had anything fun tucked away for emergencies like this, she told me the party is the best gift I could give her.

Bryan ran home to get ready and then returned with the rest of his band a little before seven. They're hanging out in the garage until we're ready to move the party out there. Zola hasn't shown up, so I figure Abigail must have called her and now I'm in double trouble. There's no time to worry about it, though. I'll have to wait until tomorrow to figure out how to fix that mess.

As Sophie's friends arrive, Isabel is great about introducing me as she greets each person. One of her friends, Dennis, comes in carrying the biggest gift bag I think I've ever seen.

After she introduces us, Isabel asks him, "What'd you get her? A new television?"

He laughs. "No." He looks around, then leans in and whispers, "It's this really awesome picture I took of her dog, Daisy. I blew it up and made it into a poster. Wait until you see it. It's the best gift ever, if I do say so myself."

"Can I see it now?" she asks him.

"No, you cannot. The birthday girl has to be the first one to see it. She's particular about those kinds of things, you know."

"She is?" Isabel asks.

"No," Dennis says. "I just like saying that word. Particular. Don't I sound really mature when I say it?"

She points Dennis to the family room so he can put his gift with the others, and after he's gone, she whispers, "That's Sophie's almost-boyfriend."

"Almost-boyfriend? As in, she likes him but he doesn't like her?"

"No, they both like each other, and they hang out all the time and talk on the phone and stuff."

"So . . . they're basically friends?"

"Yeah. But the way she talks, sometimes I think she wants to be more, you know? So, he's her almost-boyfriend in my mind."

I nod like I understand, but I'm not sure I really do.

Five minutes before seven thirty, I go through the house and shut off the lights. Then we all gather in the entryway.

"After Sophie rings the bell, Lily will go to the door," Isabel explains to everyone. "She's going to open the door really wide, and when she does, I'm going to flip on the light. As soon as the light goes on, you all yell, 'Surprise!' Until then, we have to be super quiet, so she doesn't suspect anything."

"I don't think most of the girls here know what super quiet means," I hear Dennis say.

A few people hush him.

We stand there quietly, waiting. My heart is pounding. Will she be surprised? Happy? Excited to see all of her friends in one place? Thrilled to see all the colorful packages and the delicious food?

I hope so, I hope so, I hope so.

When the doorbell finally rings, I'm shaking so bad, I can hardly make myself move. It's even worse than when I got called up to be Chef Smiley's assistant. I don't know why I'm so nervous. As I reach for the doorknob, I take a deep breath. And then I swing the door open quickly, and as I do, the lights come on and everyone yells, "Surprise!"

Sophie squeals. Isabel and I jump out and we both say, "Happy birthday," like we'd planned it, even though we hadn't. It makes us laugh and then Sophie is inside, hugging us and bouncing up and down because she's so excited.

I peek outside and see her mom wave. I wave back before I shut the door.

"I can't believe you guys did this," Sophie says, her eyes taking in the curtains of streamers and all the smiling faces.

"So, you're surprised?" Isabel asks.

Sophie laughs. "More like shocked!"

We take her into the dining room and show her

my special brownie and cookie creation. "That's so clever," she says. "How did you come up with that?"

I smile. "It's kind of a long story. I think I'll wait and tell you about it another time."

"Well, I love it."

Next we take her into the family room to show her all the gifts. Isabel says, "Lily and I have been working on this party for weeks. I was so worried you'd find out."

Sophie is beaming. She hugs us again. "Thank you guys so much. You're the best friends a girl could have." Isabel and I look at each other and smile.

"We're going to have brownie and cookie sundaes in a little while," I say. "But first, we have another surprise. A really big one that Isabel arranged. Think you can handle one more?"

She claps her hands together. "I can't wait!"

I wish I could borrow a little bit of her excitement. I'm afraid seeing the New Pirates perform might make me even sadder than seeing all of the cake pops fall apart.

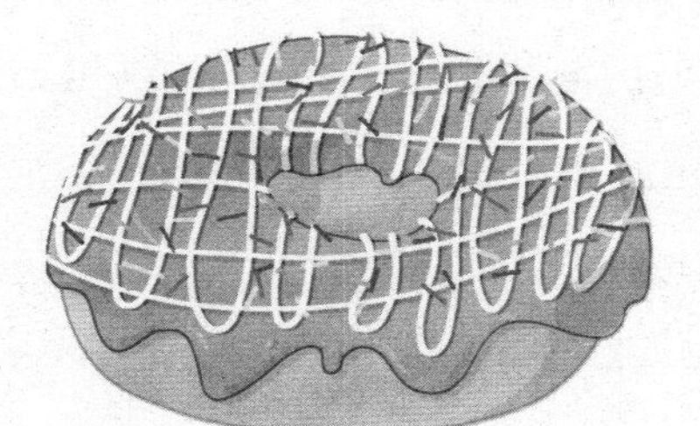

Chapter 26

dots

WHETHER A TYPE OF CANDY OR A BAND, THEY'RE PRETTY SWEET

Everyone follows Isabel and me out to the garage. When we go in, the band stops their warm-up. Sophie squeals, "Oh my gosh! You got me a *band*?"

Belinda takes the microphone and holds it like a pro. "I guess we should start by saying happy birthday, Sophie!"

The party guests clap and cheer as they gather in the middle of the garage, all eyes on the stage. Belinda puts the microphone back in the stand and picks up a black electric guitar. As she puts the strap around her neck, she says, "We're the New Pirates and we're here to give Sophie a night she won't ever forget. So let's get this party started, what do you say? Our first song is called 'This Life.'"

Sydney and Belinda start jamming on their guitars while Bryan drums out the beat. The crowd is cheering and jumping up and down.

They play and sing like they've been doing this their whole lives. It's incredible. I had no idea they were so talented. I remember what Belinda said in choir class that one day. *Without talent . . . you're nothing. You'll get nowhere.*

They definitely have talent. And they seem to be enjoying themselves too. The crowd loves them.

When they're finished, everyone raises their hands in the air and screams. Who knew twenty-five kids could make so much noise? Belinda says "Thank you" six or seven times, waiting until it's quieted down before they go into their next song.

They play one amazing song after another. Their songs are upbeat and fun and full of lyrics that are easy to remember, so by the time the chorus comes around for the third time, everyone's singing along. Like this one:

"I like you,
you like me,
that's the way
it's supposed to be."

For a whole hour, we are entertained. Dazzled. Inspired. They must practice constantly. There's no way they could be this good otherwise. I remember what Betty said to my mom when we visited Grandpa Frank, about people's dreams and how it's too easy to let things get in the way. Obviously, the New Pirates haven't let anything get in their way.

But I have.

I was trying so hard to be something I'm not—a good baker—that I didn't let myself follow my real dream. All of that time and energy should have been spent on what really matters to me. Music is what matters to me. It's what's always mattered to me.

As the show winds down, all I can think about is how badly I've messed up. I want to hug Abigail and Zola a million times over. I can only hope they'll give me another chance.

When I think the New Pirates are going to wrap up and say good night, Bryan picks up his microphone and says, "You know, I think we might have time for another song or two."

Everyone cheers.

"But I think you've heard enough from us," he says. "So I'm going to invite the Dots up here to play."

I'm looking at him, shaking my head, trying to get him to understand this won't work. I know he's trying to be nice, but I'm the only Dot who's here.

At least, I thought I was. In a matter of seconds, Abigail and Zola are on either side of me. They've been here watching? How did I not see them?

"What?" I say. "How—"

"Bryan called us," Abigail says in my ear. "He convinced us to come and play."

I give each of them a quick hug. "I'm so sorry," I tell them.

They both nod, as if to say, "We forgive you." Zola pulls her sticks from her back pocket and holds them in the air. "Let's do this thing!"

I watch as Belinda turns around and whispers something angrily to Bryan, but he pulls her off the stage. Sydney follows them.

I suddenly feel dizzy and I can hardly breathe. Is this really happening? We're actually going to play? Zola starts walking toward the stage. Abigail grabs my hand and pulls me along, the crowd parting for us as we go. I take my place at the front of the small stage, while Zola moves to the drums and Abigail picks up one of the guitars.

"First," I say, "we have a little song for the birthday girl. Happy birthday, sweet Sophie."

We break out into our fun and up-tempo version of "Happy Birthday," and the crowd claps along to the beat. It sounds really good. I look down at Sophie, standing in the front row, and I can tell she loves it.

When we finish, it feels like there are a million butterflies swarming inside my stomach. I don't think I've ever felt this nervous before. What if we can't pull off the song we wrote? What if no one likes it? The New Pirates were so good, and they've obviously practiced a lot more than we have.

I turn and look at my bandmates, and their eyes are questioning me. I bite my lip, wondering if I should just end it now. Maybe I should say, "That's all, folks," and quit while we're ahead.

But Betty's voice echoes in my brain.

The people who made their dreams come true felt afraid too, but they didn't let it stop them.

I wanted a chance to prove to Zola and Abigail that I'm committed to this band. I can show them here and now that my heart is in it a hundred percent. I messed up. I forgot what mattered most to me. This is my chance to show them who I really am.

It's my chance to show everyone. I want to be a singer.

No.

I am a singer.

I take the microphone and say, "This next song we wrote over the past few weeks. I want to play this song for you guys because I'm proud of it and I'm proud of my band. I want to say thanks to my bandmates, Zola and Abigail, for sticking with me when I let other things get in the way. I was trying to be someone I'm not.

"See, I thought I wanted to be a good baker like my friends Sophie and Isabel. The truth is, I'm a horrible baker. And maybe I'm better now than I was a month ago, but I don't even really like baking. So I'll leave the baking to the people who do like it, while I work hard on what really matters to me.

"This next song is called 'Wishing.' And tonight, my greatest wish, beyond Sophie having a great birthday, is that Abigail and Zola will forgive me. And that we have the chance to write many more songs together in the future."

I put the microphone back in the stand. I listen to my band play the introduction. And then I sing like I've never sung before.

I'm pretty sure it's the best three minutes of my entire life.

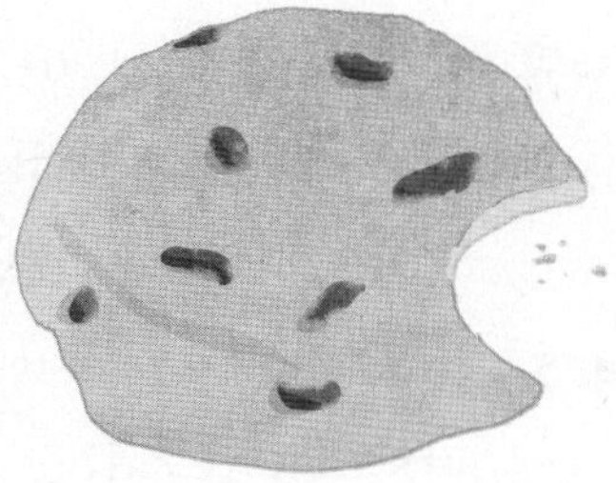

Chapter 27

music lovers cupcakes

A PERFECT HARMONY OF

CHOCOLATE AND VANILLA

There's a whole bunch of kids standing outside the choir room, waiting for Mr. Weisenheimer to announce who will be playing at the Spring Fling. Abigail and Zola are passing the time by listening to a song on Zola's iPod. They each have an earbud in one of their ears.

My gaze meets Bryan's across the sea of people. He

gives me a thumbs-up. I smile. Ever since Sophie's party, we talk almost every day. Abigail and Zola like to tease me about it, even though he's just a friend. They probably can't understand how we bonded over failed cake pops and how much it means that he helped get my band back together.

Bryan told me that when he called Abigail the day of Sophie's party, he explained how bad I felt about everything. He told her he knows what it's like to be torn in two different directions. Bryan's parents own rental property along the Oregon coast and lots of times, on the weekends, they want to drag him along with them so he can learn about home maintenance and repairs. On the one hand, he wants to help his parents, but on the other hand, his band likes to practice on the weekends, when there's not as much school stuff to worry about.

Abigail told me later that as he talked, she realized I wasn't trying to hurt anyone. I was just trying to make everyone happy. And how could she stay mad at me for something like that?

Of course, now that everyone knows the truth about my baking skills, life has been much easier.

Since the party, Abigail, Zola, and I have become a music-making machine. We wrote two more songs, and when we played them for my parents, my dad said he was honestly impressed with how far we'd come in such a short amount of time.

Our audition for the Spring Fling went well, although I was really nervous, so my voice shook a little bit. That's one thing I need to work on. Dad says it just takes practice, and some musicians get a little case of stage fright every time they have to perform. He says either I'll get over it or I'll learn to live with it. I hope he's right, because I don't ever want to stop singing.

The doors to the choir room open. Mr. Weisenheimer steps out and everyone backs up a little bit to give him some room. Zola and Abigail tear the earbuds out of their ears so they can hear what he has to say.

"Thanks for your patience, everyone," Mr. Weisenheimer says. "I want you to know, this was a really difficult decision. I said we'd have an announcement for you today by four o'clock, and here we are, a half hour late, and I apologize for that. It makes me extremely proud to work at a school with such talented musicians and singers. If I could, I'd let you all play at the Spring Fling. I truly hope all of you will decide to perform at the talent show at the end of the year. I'd love for the community to see and hear you perform."

I look at Zola and Abigail, and we all nod, as if to say, "We're in for the talent show."

Abigail squeezes my hand as we wait in agony for him to tell us who they've chosen. I'm glad he's proud of all of us, but come on, the waiting is torture!

He must read my mind because he says, "All right, enough of that. I know you're all dying to learn who will be playing at your Spring Fling. This band has some of the most talented young people I've ever seen. I can't believe they are eighth graders. I won't be surprised at all if they're touring the country someday, playing their music to millions of adoring fans.

"So, it's my pleasure to say congratulations to the New Pirates! You'll be playing at our Spring Fling this year! Let's give them a round of applause."

Everyone claps. I look over at Bryan, and now I

give him a thumbs-up. I'm truly happy for them. They totally deserve it.

"To show my appreciation to all of you for your efforts," Mr. Weisenheimer says, "come in and grab a special treat I picked up on my way to work this morning. When I called It's Raining Cupcakes a few days ago and asked if they could make something special for this occasion, they came up with some fabulous music lovers cupcakes, just for you."

We make our way into the choir room and then over to a long table, where the cupcakes are spread out along with plates and napkins. Each cupcake has vanilla frosting with a black musical note piped on top. They are gorgeous.

I grab one and slowly peel off the wrapper. The cake appears to be chocolate. I take a bite, and the way the chocolate and vanilla blend together in my mouth, it's almost magical. The chocolate flavor is different from anything I've ever tasted. It has a little bit of a spicy taste to it. Cinnamon, maybe? I don't know, but it tastes really, really good.

I turn and see Belinda standing next to me.

"Congratulations," I tell her. "I can't wait to hear you guys play again."

"Thanks. We're excited. Except I'm bummed we won't get to hear your cupcake song. Do you want to sing it for me now?" she teases.

I smile. "You know, I've learned I don't like baking cupcakes. And singing about them really isn't all that fun either. I think I'll stick to what I do best, as far as cupcakes are concerned."

And with that, I take another bite and leave to find my bandmates.

"Dudes, when do we start practicing for the talent show?" Zola asks.

Abigail and I answer at the exact same time. "Tonight!"

Chapter 28

chocolate no-bake cookies

WHATEVER WORKS,

AND THESE WORK VERY WELL

"What are you making?" Madison asks me as she saunters into the kitchen, holding her water bottle. She's wearing her uniform, off to play a game, I'm guessing.

"Chocolate no-bake cookies," I say. "The ones with the oatmeal and peanut butter. You've had them before, right?"

"I love those cookies," she says, peering into the saucepan. "Save me some, okay?"

"There's only ten of us, so there'll be some left over."

"I gotta run," she says. "Have a fun meeting."

"We will. Bye."

Today is the day I host the Baking Bookworms. Last month, when Isabel hosted, she made us little fruit tarts and lemon bars. Everyone couldn't stop talking about how good everything tasted.

But it didn't bother me.

That's who Isabel is. A wonderful baker. And today I will show the girls who I am. A girl who will make easy snacks, because they're good too, and it's okay. Whatever works, just like Chef Smiley told me.

When the dough is done, I lick the wooden spoon before I throw it in the sink.

"Sweet Uncle Pete, that's good!" I say.

"I recognize that saying," Mom says as she and Dad walk into the kitchen. "Are your no-bake cookies almost done?"

"I just need to put them on wax paper and let them set up."

"Want me to help you?" Dad asks.

"Okay. Thanks."

"How's that new song coming along?" he asks as he gets two spoons out of the drawer for us.

"We finished it and started working on another," I tell him as I scoop up a big chunk of dough.

"Wow. I'm so proud of how hard you guys have been working. How many songs are you up to?"

"Six," I tell him. "Six good ones. We wrote a couple that we ended up throwing out. They just weren't good enough."

Dad stops and looks at me. He's got a funny look in his eyes. A look that says, *I think you're going to like what I'm about to say.*

"You know, I was thinking . . ."

He waits.

I poke him in the stomach. "What? Tell me."

"Five songs is a good little set. My band's been asked to play at a company picnic coming up in June. It'll be a great venue—outside, at the park, while people mingle and eat their hamburgers and hot dogs. I'm thinking it'd be nice to have a little opening act. There'll be quite a few kids there who don't really want to hear a bunch of old fogies singing."

I drop my spoon on the counter. "Really? Dad, are you serious? You don't think they'd mind?"

"Actually, I already asked the guy who hired me," he says with a smile. "He loved the idea."

I stand on my tiptoes, throw my arms around my dad's neck, and give him a big hug. "Thank you! Abigail and Zola are going to be so excited."

The doorbell rings, interrupting our special father-daughter moment.

I pull away from Dad and check the clock. Then I look at Mom. "Uh-oh. Somebody's early."

"Go see who it is," Mom says. "Dad and I'll finish these."

I quickly wipe my hands on a towel and then head to the door. It's Sophie and Isabel and their moms.

"Hi, Lily," Sophie's mom says. "Hope it's okay we're a little early."

"Sure. Come in."

My mom comes out of the kitchen and greets the moms and asks them if they'd like some tea. They do, so they follow her back to the kitchen.

"Did you like the book *Ella Enchanted*?" Isabel asks us.

Sophie nods while I say, "I loved it. My mom did too."

"So what kinds of snacks are we having?"

I'm about to tell them about the easy things I made when the doorbell rings again. The other girls, Katie and Dharsanaa, have arrived with their moms.

"Everyone's early," Katie says. "I guess we're excited about this book!"

I lead the girls into our family room, where we'll have our discussion, while the moms visit in the kitchen.

"So, did you bake a beautiful six-layer cake, like Ella had on her fifth birthday?" Dharsanaa asks me. I can tell she's teasing me. They know that I'm not a baker, and I'm no longer afraid to admit it.

I laugh. "Um, no, there will be no homemade six-layer cake today. But I did make a cream trifle, which was mentioned in the book. We bought a pound cake, some jam and berries, and whipped cream. It was super easy to make and it looks so pretty. Wait until you see it. We layered pieces of cake, the berries, and the cream in a pretty glass bowl."

"Yum," Katie says. "That sounds good."

"And because Sophie loves chocolate," I say, "I made really easy chocolate no-bake cookies too."

"Yay!" Sophie says.

Chef Smiley was right. "Whatever works" is the best saying ever. I still have great homemade snacks and I didn't have to bake a thing.

"Are you okay with our name staying the Baking Bookworms, Lily?" Isabel asks me. "Or do you want to change it? We don't want you to feel left out."

"No, it's fine. We're all used to the name by now. You guys can do the baking. And I'll do the eating."

Everyone laughs.

Sweet Uncle Pete, I like my friends!

Chocolate No-Bake Cookies

1¾ cups sugar

4 tablespoons baking cocoa

½ cup milk

½ cup (1 stick) butter

a pinch of salt

1 tablespoon vanilla

1 cup peanut butter

3 cups quick 1-minute oats

Carefully measure out the sugar and baking cocoa into a saucepan and mix well. Slowly stir in the milk and blend well with the sugar mixture. Next, add the butter by cutting it with a knife into tablespoon-sized pats. Add a pinch of salt. Turn the burner on medium heat and stir frequently until mixture boils. Let mixture boil for two full minutes while stirring and then remove from heat. Add the vanilla and stir. Finally, add the peanut butter and oats and mix until well blended. Drop by rounded teaspoons onto a sheet of wax paper and cool. Makes about two dozen.

Strawberry Cake

Cake

1 cup (2 sticks) butter, softened

1½ cups white sugar

1 (3 oz.) package strawberry-flavored gelatin

4 eggs, room temperature

2½ cups sifted all-purpose flour

2½ teaspoons baking powder

1 cup whole milk, room temperature

½ cup strawberry puree made from frozen unsweetened strawberries

1 tablespoon vanilla

Take eggs, milk, and butter out of the refrigerator a few hours before making the batter.

Preheat oven to 350 degrees. Grease and flour two 9-inch round pans or one 9 x 13 pan.

In a large bowl, combine the butter, sugar, and strawberry gelatin. Mix on medium speed until light and fluffy. Separate the eggs; add the yolks to the batter and mix well. Whip the egg whites vigorously until soft peaks form before mixing them into the batter.

Sift flour, then measure and put into a separate bowl. Combine the baking powder with the sifted flour. Alternate adding the flour mixture and milk to the batter, mixing with each addition.

Use the blender to make a strawberry puree from a bag of frozen unsweetened strawberries. Add a little bit of water and blend until smooth. Add ½ cup puree to the batter along with the vanilla and mix well. Pour batter into prepared pans. For round pans, bake 25 to 30 minutes, for a 9 x 13, bake for 35 to 40 minutes, until a toothpick comes out clean. If you're making a layered cake, allow the cakes to cool on a wire rack for 10 minutes before removing them from the pans to cool completely.

Frosting

1 cup (2 sticks) unsalted butter, softened

8 oz. cream cheese, softened

2 teaspoons vanilla

4 cups powdered sugar

Mix butter on low until fluffy. Add cream cheese and vanilla and mix for one minute. Add powdered sugar one cup at a time, mixing thoroughly. When all powdered sugar has been added, whip the frosting on high for 30 seconds to make it nice and smooth. Spread onto cooled cake. Top with sliced strawberries, if desired.

acknowledgments

A huge thank-you to Nathalie Dion for creating such fantastic art for this book as well as for *It's Raining Cupcakes* and *Sprinkles and Secrets*. You've done an amazing job, and every time I look at the covers, I feel like I've won the cover lottery.

Thanks to Mary Hays, a fan of the first two books, who wrote to me and helped me come up with the title of this book. It's perfect!

Thanks to the amazing team at Aladdin for all your hard work and support: Bethany Buck,

Mara Anastas, Fiona Simpson, Lydia Finn, Karin Paprocki, Karina Granda, Julie Doebler, Katherine Devendorf, Andrea Kempfer, and Alyson Heller. Cupcakes for all!

A special shout-out to Jen and Katie Manullang for your support from the very beginning of this cupcake-filled journey.

Thank you to Sara Gundell for so many things, but especially for featuring my books on your blog and working your magic to get me on TV.

To the librarians and booksellers, thanks for all you do to get books into the hands of readers.

Finally, thank you to *all* you young readers who have enjoyed my books and told your friends about them. Your enthusiasm makes me over-the-moon happy, and I want you to know I appreciate you more than words can say. Keep reading!